D1264051

ROVER
YOUNGBLOOD

Books by
Thomas McAfee

POEMS & STORIES

I'LL BE HOME LATE TONIGHT

ROVER YOUNGBLOOD

ROVER YOUNGBLOOD

an American fable

by

Thomas McAfee

Ϙ Richard W. Baron
New York   1969

To Goni, Rover, the Cast,
and all of my friends.

ROVER YOUNGBLOOD

Chapter 1

IT WAS IN MAY and the reason I'd run off from my
home in Clearpoint, Alabama—the truth is, I lived
about ten mile from Clearpoint, out in the country—
was because of the mess I'd got into with pa and some
other things. He wasn't what you'd call a bad man but
he was always beating on me and I was sixteen year old
and getting tired of it. You're getting to be a man about
that time and you want to be treated like a man.

Another part of the reason for me running off had to
do with this gal, which I'll get to in a minute. About a
week before I left they was having a dance over at Clearpoint. Clearpoint ain't much of a town but it's the only
one I'd ever been to then, so it seemed pretty big to me.
There was two drugstores, three dry good stores, two
markets, and so on. And then they had a big American
Legion hall made out of white stone slabs where there

was a dance every Saturday night. I'd nearly always go if pa would let me. Sometimes I'd ride my mare, Bessie, and sometimes I'd walk.

I met this gal, Sandra Jean, over there one night. It's hard to tell how she looked but to me when I first seen her she was about the nicest-looking gal I'd ever looked at. She had yellow-colored hair that hung down to about the middle of her back. Her body was filled out like a real woman.

At first I thought she was just another gal, no matter how good-looking she was, but after a week or two I started courting her heavy and then I got to taking her to church on Sunday nights, which means where I lived that you're next thing to getting engaged. Taking her to church was all right with pa, because of what ma said. "Any boy that's got his heart in the right place, believes in God Almighty, goes to church regular and I don't care with who—he's heading in the right direction." Ma trusted people more than she had a right to but I think if you can do it that way you're better off. Ma was what you'd call good, straight through.

Pa wasn't religious and always said he didn't hold to anything but the Bible itself and said he didn't want to hear no preacher trying to tell him what the Bible meant. "Looka here," he'd say, "one says to sprinkle and one says to duck. Got some of these that tell you to handle snakes. How do they know more'n I know. I learnt to read and can read as good as any of them preachers." Another thing he said was that a preacher charges you to listen to him.

Ma was different. I can't remember she ever missed a single Sunday at Shady Grove Church. She'd take part of her eggs money every Sunday and put it in the collection plate. "Your pa is sinful but means well," she'd tell me, and she'd pray for him every night. Because of ma's feelings I could go to Sunday-night service with Sandra Jean. (I thought that was a pretty name and one time I asked her how she got it. Her ma read a article in the *Progressive Farmer* about this young gal named Sandra that had a dog that pulled her in out of the river when she was drowning, and her ma thought it was a nice name. She couldn't remember where her ma got the Jean.)

Sandra Jean and me would sit on the back row of the church house and pass notes to each other about how much we loved each other. Then afterwards we'd go down in the woods back of the church and outhouses and court. This kept up for a good while and finally Sandra Jean got to talking about us getting married. This here was something to think about, I told her. Me without nothing but one suit of clothes, three pair of overalls, one white shirt, two work shirts, underwear and socks, and my mare, Bessie. Pa claimed the mare for his own because he said he'd fed it. It was mine, though, because I'd took care of it and nursed it back to health when it was a colt.

I said, "Sandra Jean, we got to wait a while. It ain't that I don't love you or nothing like that but pa would skin me alive if I was to get married, for one thing, and another thing we'd be having younguns coming along and I couldn't feed them much less you and me."

Another thing I didn't tell her was that Jimmy Lunsford told me about a week before that he'd courted about as heavy as I had. He said he'd got him a piece

3

four or five times and Sandra Jean wanted to marry him too. Jimmy Lunsford might of been telling a big lie because he always use to be bragging about how much tail he got.

Back to why I run off from home. After this Saturday-night dance me and Sandra Jean got on my mare and rode out towards my house to Tolbert Addison's to pick up a bottle of homebrew. Tolbert sells cheap to his friends and I've been a friend of his all my life. Then we rode out to west pasture, set down under some pine trees, and started to drink the homebrew and court.

We was talking about the dance, this and that, how tacky she thought Naydene Adderholt was who was at the dance and always flirting with everybody that had on pants. After we'd drank about half the bottle, Sandra Jean said, "How much do you love me?"

"A whole lot," I told her.

"Naw," she said, "I want you to tell me just exactly how much."

"More'n any other girl I know of."

"Enough to marry me?"

"We done talked about that," I said. "I ain't got no land and I don't know nothing about town work."

"I think maybe I'm gonna have a little baby," she said and her voice sounded like she was about to bawl.

I turned up the bottle of homebrew and took me a long swallow. "How do I know I'm its daddy?"

"Whatta you mean?" Sandra Jean asked me. "Course you're its daddy. Who else?"

"What about Jimmy Lunsford?"

That just about got her. She couldn't say nothing for a while but just sniffed, and then all of a sudden she

4

started telling me what a low-down, mean son of a bitch
I was for taking advantage of a pore innocent girl like
her and how she never did want to do it with me in the
first place except that she loved me so much and that
was the only way she could show me how much she loved
me. Well, we got into a long argument, Sandra Jean
cried, then we got all right again and by that time I was
feeling so high on the homebrew I didn't much care if
she was gonna have a litter.

"Listen here," I said and I put my mouth up to her
neck, "we can talk about this tomorrow or sometime."
Then we laid there on the pine needles.

Finally I took her home and crawled in beside my
brother Ed about three o'clock A.M. I didn't feel much
like getting up at four to help pa with the milking and
feeding. I was still high and pa could tell.

"What time did you get in?" pa wanted to know in the
barn when I was throwing down hay from the loft.

"About midnight," I said.

"I know when you got in." He stood there looking up
at me, his hands on his hips. "You been drinking that
homebrew and you're still drunk. Ain't you?"

"Nawsir."

But he could tell I was and I knew it.

"Come down here to me," he said. He was taking off
his belt.

Pa was a big man, about six foot two, weighed about
two hundred and ten. He had a red face and a thick neck
and he was stronger'n a mule.

"I ain't gonna take no beating from you," I said. "I'm
sixteen year old and I ain't gonna take no beating from
you."

"You're a young son of a bitch," he hollered at me. He didn't mean nothing against ma, I know, but he always said that when he got mad.

I started down the ladder and when he could reach me he started swinging his leather belt at my legs. I jerked around and jumped on top of him and hit him a couple of times in the face. It wasn't long before he was on top of me and I got a real good beating. He weighed about fifty pounds more than I did.

Finally I was laying there on the ground with blood running out of my nose and pa said, "Go to the house and wash yourself up. Then come on back here and help me finish the feeding."

Ma was in the house making biscuit dough and heard me pulling well water and washing on the porch. She come to the screen door and saw my face.

"You and your pa been at it?"

I nodded yes and she started to cry.

Pa wasn't anybody to take nothing from anybody. I had two brothers—Ed and Silas—and two sisters—Lamour Anne and Naomi. He didn't whip the gals but they was scared to death of him.

I wouldn't talk to pa for the rest of the time till I run off. He was the main reason I did it but I wouldn't say nothing bad against pa till today. The other reason I run off was Sandra Jean. Maybe that youngun was Jimmy Lunsford's or maybe somebody else. Maybe there wasn't a youngun to begin with and she was lying. I don't know how I could of found out and I didn't much care.

One thing about pa, I don't think he was scared of the devil but I think he was half scared of ma because he thought she had a close connection with God.

6

Chapter 2

SO I LEFT HOME the next night. I didn't go to sleep a bit, then got up about two-thirty A.M. I tried to be quiet because ma was such a light sleeper and she would of pitched a fit if she'd woke up.

After I'd put my shoes and socks on, I set there on the side of the bed and looked at my room by the moonlight that was coming in my windows. Brother Ed was laying on the other side of the bed, sleeping and snoring a little. Brother Silas, younger than me and Ed, was on a cot by one of the windows.

I was a little sad thinking I might not ever see this room again that I was raised up in. Over the chester-drawers was my shotgun (me and Ed owned it together, so I didn't take it with me). Then there was a picture of Sandra Jean on the washstand and she had wrote with a fountain pen: "Best wishes till the day I die." I decided not to take it along since Sandra Jean was partly why I was leaving. On the wall me and Ed had hung up two rabbit skins and three snake rattlers. That's about all I had in that room except my clothes.

Well, I said to myself, you can't set here the rest of your life and think about what you done in the past. I put on some overalls and a work shirt, then put the rest of my clothes, including my Sunday shoes, in a chicken-feed sack I'd got the night before out of the kitchen. Ma had washed it out and pressed it with an iron.

I said to myself, Good-bye, Ed, Good-bye, Silas, then stepped over Silas and got out the window. At the barn I saddled up Bessie but didn't get on her till I'd led her a piece down the road.

That night laying in bed I'd decided to head for Manfred City, a place I never had been before, but it was suppose to be a big place and anybody I ever talked to that had been there always bragged about it. They said it had about forty thousand people and I couldn't even think of that many. Clearpoint didn't have but about five hundred, not counting the niggers.

"Bessie," I said, "me and you is headed for a big adventure."

I turned around and looked back at the home place. It wasn't any fine house but I never had much kick against it. Two rooms on each side of a porch that went straight through the middle. The house was set up on sandstone chunks, and when me and Ed was little we'd play under there.

That's where I spent my life, I said to myself. Besides my brothers I was leaving, I was leaving also: Lamour

Anne, Naomi, even pa—but especially ma. She'd probably cry a whole lot and pray for me.

I said, "Old farmhouse, so long." Then to Bessie, "Giddap." Off we went.

The road was gravel with big gullies on the side of it and the cars couldn't hardly pass if they was any cars but it was a good road for a horse. The furtherest I'd ever been down that road was about ten mile because there wasn't anyplace to go unless you was going to Manfred City, which was seventy mile off.

When the sun started coming up I got so full of myself I wanted to slap Bessie on the butt and say, "Go fast as hell, honey," and I wanted to stand up in the stirrups, hold on with one hand to Bessie's mane and let out a big holler. *Looka here, morning, I'm gonna ride straight into you. I'm gonna tear you apart and love you to death.*

The sky was like the sky of a calendar ma had in the kitchen: pink, yellow, purple mingling, and not a cloud. It was so nice it didn't look natural but like somebody had taken a brush and painted it by hand.

I felt good like that for a couple of hours but then I got to studying about what I was gonna do for food. Once I got to Manfred City I could work and make some money but what was I gonna do till then? Maybe I could stop at houses along the way and do chores. If they was any houses.

About midmorning when the sun was coming down strong Bessie started to sweat: thick white foam was rising along where the saddle wore on her and where my legs rubbed against her belly. I started to sweat too. The bushes along the side of the road—mainly sassafras and

9

scrubby oak and weeds—they was all coated over white with dust and made you hot just to look at them. Sometimes over on the sides of the road past the gullies and the bushes you'd see stumpland where people had sold off all their timber, sometimes you'd see a old wood house that had fell apart and there wasn't anything standing but the chimney, sometimes wore-out farmland that had gullies crissing and crossing through it. It wasn't much scenery to look at and it even made you feel bad to see it.

Finally I said to Bessie, "I'm getting thirsty and so're you. We got to slow down and take it gentle till we spot us a farmhouse."

I wiped my head with a handkerchief and started to sing. It made me want water more, but one thing is this: singing helps take your mind off of your troubles.

I knew all the words to this song we would sing on Sunday night over at Shady Grove:

> Jesus has a telescope
> And it's straight on you.
> He can see everything
> That you ever do.

> If it's big or little
> He can sight you in.
> Think of that telescope
> When you start to sin.

Then the chorus went:

> He's got you covered
> You hateful infidel,

And he can send you
Right straight to hell.
And he can send you
Right straight to hell.

I never had thought much about the words to that
song because I never was much religious and I went to
church mainly to court, but I had seen a lot of religious
people. Ever once in a while when the crowd would get
to shouting and washing each other's feet, I'd get religious too—or I reckon that's what it was, but I
wouldn't feel it very long.

Once ma come running to the back of the church,
crying, and wanted me to come down front and confess.
She would always sit on the first or second row. I didn't
know what to confess except sometimes I would drink
homebrew and I'd had me poontang a good many times
and sometimes I'd played with myself in the hayloft. I
couldn't tell none of these things in the church house.

Ma kept pulling at my sleeve and crying and telling
me to come on down and confess for my old mother and
for God. I didn't know what to do because of the way
ma was acting, so I finally let her lead me down to the
preacher. I got down on my knees and told him I smoked
rabbit tobacco and said cuss words sometimes.

He prayed for me and then they was a good deal of
shouting and Amen. When it was all over I took my
gal down behind the church house and we courted.
That's the way it was: getting religion wouldn't last
long for me.

I was thinking about all this when I was riding along
there on Bessie, and I decided I was either a backslider

11

or else I never had been anywhere to backslide. The way everybody talked and went on about God, it made him sound ugly and mean, like he didn't want anybody to enjoy theirself or do anything else much that was any account. I said to myself, Now what is the sense of praying to anybody like that? And another thing, some of the most religious folks at Shady Grove Church was also some of the meanest folks I knew of.

Take Grady Tull, who was a big, red-faced man and had black hair. He would footwash every Sunday night, and he could holler "I've sinned" louder than anybody in church. You'd think from all the commotion he made that he was about as good as anybody, or else he was headed in the right direction from here on out. But Grady had this girl named Truby that he would let us schoolboys have for a quarter apiece. Truby was on the fat side and had a red face like her old man's, but besides that she was all right. The main thing about Truby was she was eighteen year old. We would set down in the Tulls' living room, maybe six or seven of us, and talk to Grady Tull while we waited.

They had a right nice living room: a linoleum floor, a couch that Grady said you could make out into a bed, and some pictures on the wall. We'd talk and wait till our turn. Mrs. Tull always stayed back in the kitchen and acted like she didn't know there was any visitors around. Then when it was our turn we'd give Grady a quarter and go in the bedroom. Me and Ed would sell scrap iron and Coca-Cola bottles to get our quarter.

We had some other religious people about as bad as him, but they didn't sell their own younguns for a quarter. I stopped thinking about religion for a while and got to thinking about Truby and about how I probably never would crawl in bed with her again. Right then I spotted a farmhouse.

Chapter 3

A FARMHOUSE as a farmhouse don't mean much, probably wouldn't make the next man stop to think about it, but a farmhouse when you're hot and thirsty and your mare's hot and thirsty too—that makes a big difference.

It's funny about this farmhouse I spotted, because before I spotted it I'd been thinking about religion. Well, this farmhouse had its own special kind of religion—a kind I never had seen in my life before.

The house was setting back from the road, up on a little hill. A trail led through some bushes and briars to the front porch, and it was up high on chunks of sandstone so you could crawl under it. It was higher up than my home place that I'd just left. The house looked to have four rooms or thereabouts, and it was the gray color of a mole's fur. It wasn't the worst-looking house

I ever saw, but it wasn't kept up the way ma would keep up a house.

I couldn't see no sign of life, but me and Bessie made our way along the path. One thing I could see, though, was a well covering out in back, and that looked good to me. You can get thirsty and you can drink all the soda pop or homebrew or anything else you want to, but you can't beat water. I always heard ma say that, and it's the truth. She didn't mention the homebrew.

Up close to the porch I could see all kinds of junk scattered in the weeds—old rusted car fenders and pieces of dresses and a man's hat that was faded and out of shape and some broke fruit jars and old shoes and all the like.

I hitched Bessie to the steps and went up on the porch and knocked. The wood doors was open but the screens was shut.

I waited a minute and didn't anybody come, and then I started to hear a kind of moaning sound. I knocked again, this time harder. After a minute or two a man come to the door. It was hard to make him out through the screen, but it looked like he was dressed up in white clothes.

"What you-uns want?" he said. He had a voice that was low-pitched but at the same time it would carry.

"I want to get a drink of water if I can. And some for my mare."

"Whur do you come from?"

"Close to Clearpoint."

"I ain't never heared of it." It didn't sound much like he cared where I come from or anything else.

15

"We been riding since about two-thirty this morning and we ain't had no water," I said to him.

He stood there looking at me for a while. He could see me, but I couldn't see him except for the white. I was about ready for him to tell me to get off of his land and stay off.

Then all of a sudden he said to me, "Come on in the house and don't let no flies in. We're right in the middle of a prayer meeting."

At Shady Grove Church they always had prayer meeting on Wednesday night. Ma would go and so would my sisters. So it seemed to me funny they was having prayer meeting right in the middle of the day, but I went on in the house. It was dark in there and it took me a little bit to get so I could see. The man did have on white, like I said. It was long underwear.

His face was dark and thin and it made you think he didn't eat enough, or if he did, that whatever he ate didn't go to his face. He had a lot of black hair that was oily and stringy and hung down to the sides of his face. Then he had these eyes that was black as you ever seen but white as you ever seen around the black. I had the feeling of him more like a animal than a man. I said to myself, You better watch out for this one because he looks like the kind you and your brother Ed might catch in a trap.

We were in what looked like the living room. Two cane-bottom chairs was by the fireplace, and the fireplace had a Vicks Salve sign in front of it. There was a lot of religious sayings on hand-painted signs on the walls. BE YE KIND ONE TO ANOTHER. LIFE IS ONE THING BUT DEATH IS ANOTHER. THE DEVIL IS RIGHT BEHIND YOU. And so on. I

16

was taking all this in while he was looking me up and down.

"My name is Lord Jesus Turner," he said and put out his hand. "You been saved?"

I told him my name was Rover Youngblood and I didn't know whether I'd been saved or not.

"If you'd of been saved, boy, you'd know it. It ain't nobody—man, woman, or child—that don't know if he's been saved." He squinted at me like he was trying to look right inside me. "Turn around here to the light and let me see your face good. I can tell by a face if the soul and heart's been saved or not."

He turned me around so I was facing the screen door and got up close to me and looked. He'd turn my face this way and then that way, and finally he said:

"Naw, you ain't been saved. You ain't been saved no more'n a catfish. I can see in your eyes and in your teeth and even in the way your hair stands. You ain't been saved. You ain't even started to be saved. Shoot!" he said, and when he said it you could see all of his front teeth or what was left. A couple to the one side was gone and the others was sharp like spikes. He wasn't a purty man, I'll tell you that.

He went on: "I reckon I'll have to work on you. Where you headed for?"

"Manfred City," I told him.

He moved back and raised his right hand like he was going to slap me, only I could tell by the way he did it that he wasn't going to slap me.

"God lives here. God lives there. God lives everywhere. Even in the hellholes. And that's a hellhole. A hellhole is full of the snakes of the devil. About near anyplace you go to is a hellhole. You need God, son. Son, how can you live without God?"

I was trying to think up a good answer when I heard a woman's voice behind the shut door in the next room.

"What you awaitin on?" the woman's voice said.

"A sinner's come to my door," Lord Jesus Turner said.

"I'm in here on my knees. Bring him on in."

"He ain't been saved. I can't take him in there to the Shrine of the Holiness without him saved. Come on out here, Virgin."

"I'll say Amen," she said, and then I heard her holler Amen.

"You turn around," he told me. "I ain't gonna have you look at the Shrine of the Holiness and you unclean."

I turned around till I heard the door open and shut, and then Lord Jesus said, "Now you can look."

Well, I did. Here was this woman that he called the Virgin standing there in a long white dress that looked like it was made out of bleached flour sacks. She must of stood six and a half foot tall, a good seven inches taller than Jesus Christ. She had about the ugliest woman-face I ever saw. The chin come off square and the eyes was set way back in her head. It was nearly black all around her eyes. Then she had long hair that hung down her back and over her shoulders.

"My name is Virgin Turner," she said and put her hands on her hips like she'd knock me down if I said it wasn't. On her dress, right about where her belly button should have been, was a red heart pinned on.

"I'm Rover Youngblood," I said. I thought I might as well get the whole story over with right quick. "I come

18

from close to Clearpoint and I'm set out for Manfred City. Me and my mare named Bessie needs some water. I'd be happy to do some chores to get me a meal."

Lord Jesus said, "Virgin, look at his face."

She come up close, looked down at me, and I got inspected again.

"I know you can't tell like I can tell about the unclean," Lord Jesus said, "but even you oughta be able to tell about this boy."

"He ain't fit for Heaven," she said. "You can tell it in his eyes, the way they zag around."

I didn't know what to think, them looking at me the way they was and talking about me like I wasn't there, and another thing I didn't know what to think was the way they was got up and their names.

"Only thing is," Lord Jesus said and stood back from me and frowned, "I can feed you if you'll let me save you."

I didn't like the sound of that a bit. I didn't think he could save me anyhow.

"How far is it from here to Manfred City?" I asked him.

"It's a long ways off and like I said before it's hot with the devil. Ain't it, Virgin?"

She bucked her head up and down.

Lord Jesus went on talking: "Me and the Virgin held us a street revival up there at Manfred City. Two year ago. Got us twenty-five converts on one Saturday night. Made us two hunnert dollars to carry on the Lord Jesus' work. A old woman come up to us that hadn't prayed in seventeen year. She was drunk as a dog but she come up to me in front of the Red Dot Store and wanted me to

19

teach her how to pray. I told her to give me whatever it was she had in her pocketbook to swig on, and she come out with a half pint of homebrew. I poured it out and watched it mingle in the dirt. That's the kind of a thing me and the Virgin do."

He stopped a little bit and got his breath. He was talking in a mournful voice.

"Tears come to the old woman's eyes like tears come to a baby's eyes when she seen her only friend broke on the dirt before her. I said to her, 'Old woman, go forth renewed.' Me and the Virgin sprinkled her, and she done it. She went forth renewed. She went forth in the name of the Cordial Church, the Lord Jesus Turner, and the Virgin Turner. Ain't it so, Virgin?"

"Amen." She said it loud and bucked her head up and down again.

I'd about decided the Lord Jesus wasn't gonna stop. Part of the time while he was talking he held his head back on his neck with his adam apple sticking out and his eyes about half shut. He looked like he was in some kind of a dream or getting ready for a fit.

"You set down right here," Lord Jesus said and pointed to one of the cane-bottom chairs, "and me and the Virgin'll put on some civilian clothes. She'll cook you up some dinner."

They went off to the back room, not the side one they called the Shrine of Holiness.

Chapter 4

I SET LOOKING at the signs on the walls that was painted with different colors on boards cut off of new lumber. Some of the signs I hadn't already read was these:

YOU NEED ME. I NEED YOU. LET'S GET TOGETHER.

PRAY EVERYDAY.

SHELL OUT TO JESUS.

WHAT WOULD YOUR MOTHER THINK?

The living room was a lot fancier than ours back at Clearpoint. I don't mean it was nicer or kept up better, because you couldn't find anybody to keep up a place better than ma, but this place was just fancier. They had a big deep chair that was yellow and lace pieces was on the arms of it, and they had a sewing machine but it was stacked up with old newspapers and magazines on it and looked like it hadn't been used in a long time. Tall as the Virgin was I didn't see how she could get her legs under it to pump it anyhow. Another thing, on the mantel there was a big picture in a frame of the Virgin and Jesus Christ, them holding a cross between them.

I was still looking around when Lord Jesus and the Virgin come out of the back room. I mean they was dressed up. They was fit for anything. He had on a black suit with a black coat that hit him about the knees. They both done a couple of show-off turnabouts. On the back of his coat there was a big white cross sewed on, and it looked like it was strips of sheet. The Virgin had on a black dress that come all the way down to the floor like her white dress did; embroidered on the back of it in white was this: I'M A VIRGIN.

"How you like it?" she asked me.

"It looks nice," I said.

"I bought this here dress in Birmingham. One time when me and Lord Jesus was on a revival. Got the embroider work done at Manfred City. A old lady that got saved done it for me."

She whirled around so the dress flared up and you could see her legs. They was skinny and bony.

"Son," the Lord Jesus said and leaned back against the mantelpiece, "these here is our civilian clothes. Black. So we can meet the corruption of the world." He rubbed on his coat and went on: "Me and the Virgin don't believe you can have the sanctity of white rub up agin ever no-good, no-count trash that comes along. There in the Shrine of Holiness we put on white when we turn to God. But out here with civilians we wear black to match the civilians." He stopped and turned around to his wife. "Cook up me and this boy some

22

dinner." Then he turned right back around to me and said: "Come on."

The Virgin turned around and went to the back of the house, and me and Lord Jesus went outdoors, down the steps.

"This here's my mare Bessie," I said and patted her on the flank.

"It's a good many of animals that's a lots better'n man. This here mare is free of sin and I can tell it by the way her eyes is set." He backed off from Bessie and squatted down. Then he held up his thumb and finger like he was measuring Bessie's eyes. "Yessir, her eyes is set good. What you say you call her?" He didn't wait for me to answer. "Man had oughta learn to save his soul by watching the dumb beast of field and stream."

Bessie shifted her feet some because it didn't look like she wanted to be inspected any more than I did.

"Bessie's a good little mare," I told Lord Jesus. "I raised her up from when she was a colt."

He didn't seem to be listening to me. He never did seem to be listening, or if he did it didn't much seem like he cared a flitter about what you was saying. What it looked like was this, that he was always thinking about what he was gonna say next.

"You got a bucket so I can water her?"

"Bring her on to the barn." He gave a hitch with his thumb.

We got to the back of the house and he told me to draw up some water from the well. I drunk down about four gourd dippers of that water before I quit.

"Boy, ain't nothing on earth, not homebrew, Coca-Cola, strawberry soda water or what, that tastes as good as fresh well water when you're thirsty," I told Lord Jesus.

"Come on," he said and we went on towards the barn. It was down a little hill.

The barn wasn't very big, two stalls, a hallway, and a loft. It didn't have any livestock in it. What it did have was a pretty red car that looked new.

"That there is sumpin," I told him. "Boy howdy. That there musta cost you lots of money."

He stood there for a little bit with his hands on his hips and looking at his car. His mouth turned up at the sides and his eyes slitted off so he was smiling. It looked like he was some kind of a animal that had got what it was after and was so happy about it, all it could do was just stand there with its hands on its hips and say, Looka there what I got.

"Lemme show you," he said and we went through the hallway to the car. "This here is what you call a convertible car. That means you can take the top off of it if you want to. I bet you ain't never seen a car like this here one before."

I started to tell him I never had seen such a car, but he didn't give me a chance to say it. What I was thinking was, If you had a car with a top on it, why would you want to take it off?

He kept on talking: "This here car has got a radio, a heater to keep you warm in the winter time when it gets cold, and winders that will go up and down and all you got to do is push on a button. This here car was paid for by God, is used for God's service, and is blessed by God. Name of Lord Jesus. The reason it's such a good car is because of all that. Looka here."

He went towards the back of the car and I followed
him, and there on the back of the car was wrote with
white paint: BE CORDIAL TO LORD J. AND VIRGIN.

"Now then, boy, prepare yourself. I'm gonna show
you the miracles of the world performed in the name of
God."

Then he got in the car and started up the motor.
After a minute or two all kinds of things started happening so it looked like that car was gonna come apart. The
windows got to going up and down, and the top started
rolling back and making a growling sound, and about
the time the top had got all the way back some music
commenced to play.

"Shit, that's sumpin," I said before I remembered how
religious he was. He couldn't hear me because of all the
racket that was going on.

"What do you think?" he hollered at me.

"That there is a doozie," I hollered back at him.

Let me tell you it was, because I never had saw the
likes of it before. There wasn't nothing in Clearpoint
like that and probably never would be. My ma would of
called it the work of the devil instead of the work of
God. Ma didn't like things that she thought was not
necessary, and she didn't like things that she thought
was show-off. Maybe it was because she hadn't got around
the world enough, I don't know.

"Get in on the other side," Lord Jesus hollered at me.

I did. The seat was so easy you sunk right down into
it, nearly like a feather bed.

"Now push on that button there."

I'd push it one way and the window would go up, and
another way and the window would go down.

I was about to ask Lord Jesus what made the window do like that but when I looked over at him he was leaned back in the seat with his eyes closed.

"What a glory it is to be Lord Jesus," he said out loud but I didn't think it was to me. His mouth hung open, and from the way he looked I got the feeling he liked that car better than anything on earth including the Virgin.

After a while he opened his eyes and said, "Get out. We gonna run down the battery."

He got the top down and shut all the windows tight.

"You know what I call her?" he said to me.

I shook my head that I didn't.

"Dreama. It's from Dreama Glory. She's my earthly sweetheart and the dream of what's to come. The Virgin's my sweetheart of the Shrine of the Holiness. You want some homebrew?"

I must have give him a quick look—me thinking about him being so religious and talking about corruption.

He seen the look I give him and said, "I take it for spiritual purposes. I bless it first. Wouldn't any homebrew blessed by me do anything but good. One thing, it puts you in closer contact with the One, the Two, and the Three. That makes up me."

I followed him out of the barn and he leaned up against the side of it. He took a red handkerchief and wiped the sweat off of his face.

"You drink homebrew that's blessed and you can get to know yourself better. Gettin to know yourself better can get you saved. Some people swig homebrew just to swig it and don't care what it does. I swig it to be spir-

26

itual. Why, in the olden days I turned the water to wine. You can read it in the Bible."

He had his hand up over his eyes to cut off the glare. I knew with all that getup he had on he must of been awful hot.

He pointed to some woods down back of the barn—a lot of pine trees mainly. "Down yonder," he said, "in them woods is where I get my homebrew. Niggers make it. We'll go down there in a minute and get some. They make it and I bless it. I bless theirs too, so I get mine free."

The woods was too thick for me to see any houses.

Chapter 5

WE WALKED DOWN a hill of pasture that had a water branch at the bottom of it. Not much of a branch because it was growed up with weeds.

"Sometimes I get sprinkling water out of here," the Lord Jesus told me. "Seems like it's more natural and like the Bible than well water. The Lord God that is me put it here when the world was created and the well was dug by the hands of man that is sinful to begin with because of the Garden of Eden."

I wanted to know if everything that was made by the hands of man was sinful. I was thinking of the clothes I had on and my old man's barn and my ma's milk churn—if all such as this was sinful.

"It shore is if I don't bless it. I can't get around to each and every city and farm in the country." The Lord Jesus Turner pulled the top off of a weed and started to chewing on it. "What I can do, though, to help folks out is to bless without me on the spot. Like if a woman was to say to me that she's got this here sister over towards Rodesia, Mississippi, with a herd of cattle and wants them blessed. I could bless them right here on the spot and them not be tainted no more. Or on the other hand, if her sister at Rodesia, Mississippi, was to send me a postcard and want me to bless the cattle, I could do that. I've blessed as far off as Germany and Old Mexico."

We was walking through tall weeds now and not too far from where the woods was to begin. They was thick with a lots of undergrowth between the tree trunks.

He kept on: "Them that seek is going to get helped by me, along with my assistant, the Virgin. Them that don't, don't care and will pass on to the torment that is spoke of in Revelations. Take you: you come to my door by horse because they was something in your soul said come to my door, and that you would be saved, like as not. *You* didn't know it but your soul that's got the whisperin voice of a two-day-old baby said for you to come. Same as these here niggers off in these woods come to me to be saved. And they stay right here. They won't go off to *De*troit. They got sense."

Right now we was up to the trees. I was getting ready to follow the Lord Jesus but he put his hand on my shoulder and said to me: "You-uns better wait right here. They might not want you to see their secret city. One time a white man busted into their secret city and they cut off his head and stuck it on a pole because they figgered he hadn't been saved. Oli-Oli can tell who's saved because I learned him how to tell."

He was making me want to look at the secret city, and

why in the thunder did he bring me off down here if he wasn't gonna let me look?

"Who is this Oli-Oli?" I asked the Lord Jesus Turner.

"He is a old nigger man that is high above a hunnert years of age. He has got a special insight to contact with me. When I first knowed him, he was a witch doctor and wild as a savage out of the heart of Africa. Then I up and saved him and he's one of my best converts. Now you stay right here. I won't be gone no time."

Lord Jesus went over to our left a little bit and they was a path he took that went winding. It wasn't long till he was out of sight. I stood for a while and then I set. I got to thinking about somebody cutting off your head and putting it on a stick because you wasn't saved. What if some of them niggers was to come out of the woods and see me. They'd like as not tell me what the Lord Jesus said: they could tell by my eyes that I wasn't saved and fit for Heaven, and then they'd like as not cut off my head with a ax and stick it on a pole. They might eat my body or throw it to the hogs. I was gonna stay as quiet as I could.

On about fifteen-twenty minutes the Lord Jesus hadn't come back yet and I got to studying that maybe they had took off his head. The old witch doctor might of lost his faith and went back to a savage. I caught a big green grasshopper that I held for a while. Then I let him go and listened to hear something but I couldn't hear a thing but birds and insects and the like.

I reckon I waited on thirty minutes more and Lord Jesus Turner still hadn't come so I said to myself: Rover Youngblood, head chopped off or not, you may as well go on and look at the secret city and Oli-Oli that use to be a savage and a witch doctor and see what they done to the Lord Jesus. It may be the last time you get such a chance and dead or alive you can say that you seen it.

So I got up off the ground and started on the winding path. Either side of me it was so thick you couldn't see no distance. I walked for five minutes or ten minutes— I don't know—and finally come to where it was beginning to clear some. Then I taken a sharp turn on the path and right smack they was this clearing and what I seen I never had seen before.

It was the secret city!

It was something. They was nine houses about the same size that circled the clearing—made out of old Vicks Salve signs and soda pop signs and rusted tin and old lumber. Big gaps in the walls would let in the fresh air. Then one big house was made out of the same kind of thing, and it had a upstairs that looked like a barn loft. Here and yonder on the ground would be a truck tire filled up with dirt and petunias and other kinds of flowers growing in it. Pathways went up to the doors of the houses and led off to the other houses and the main house. They was lined off with fruit jars stuck about halfway mouth-down in the dirt. Everything was neat and looked like in a magazine.

Now as to the niggers that lived in the secret city. Nearly all the grownups was inside the main house or standing outside the door, moaning and taking on and shifting from one foot to the other like they was rocking. Some of the younguns was there too but most was playing in the dirt that looked like it was swept with a sage broom. Sometimes somebody would let out a holler, sometimes a loud Amen. I thought maybe it might be

31

because the Lord Jesus Turner was blessing the homebrew. It turned out it was.

The main thing that hit me was how the people was
got up in their clothes. The Lord Jesus and Virgin didn't
come close to their getup because they mainly didn't
wear a thing and was nearly neckid. The younguns was
as neckid as a jaybird and didn't mind to scratch or do
anything else anywhere they took a notion to. The
women had pieces of cloth—all different colors and
bright colors, like you would find in a nice quilt—in a
little V around the private parts. Their tits and all else
was right there for the world to see. Most of the men-
folks had their privates covered with cloth like the
women but some of them was just hanging there.

The whole business looked like you was in another
world and I said to myself, What would the folks in
Clearpoint say? I said, What would my ma say? But I
put it right out of my mind because she would of
dropped dead. Rover Youngblood, I went on to myself,
they's a good deal goes on that you don't see in Clearpoint.

Finally my eyes come to land on a stake that had a
skull on it. Near the main house. Then another one and
another one. They was five in all. Five people not saved
and was unlucky enough to come wandering through
the secret city.

I was scared and about to turn and run off when right
then one of the neckid younguns playing in the dirt
spotted me and started blabbering in what sounded like
a unknown tongue. They all started walking towards
me, not fast, and it didn't seem like I could move. All I
could think of was my head up on a stick.

As they was getting close to me a man about five foot and neckid except for wearing a band around his head with turkey feathers in it pushed his way through to the front. He looked over a hundred year of age because he was wrinkled like a old Irish potato that has set in the dark too long. Then when they was about fifteen foot away the Lord Jesus Turner pushed in front of the old man. Lord Jesus was wearing his long underwear.

Later on he told me he had took off his black civilian clothes because he was among the saved and besides he was blessing the homebrew.

I have got to say one thing. I was happy to see the Lord Jesus Turner.

Chapter 6

"BE YE KIND ONE TO ANOTHER!" the Lord Jesus hollered as loud as he could.

All of them savages was mulling around me and making a storm of racket that hornets would of been afraid of. Oli-Oli was all bent over and dancing a kind of jig and he would stick out a finger ever now and then and poke me in the stomach.

Lord Jesus was standing right beside me and he had his right arm raised up in the air with the palm out.

"Be ye kind one to another! Be ye kind one to another!" and then, "Remember we got to drank the blessed homebrew before the blessing raises out of it."

Oli-Oli heard that because he come up from his crouch and held out his arms like a eagle. I figured then Oli-Oli could understand something beside the unknown

34

tongue. At least he could understand American. All of them got quiet, including the neckid younguns.

Lord Jesus clapped his hands in the air and said something that sounded like Flu Flu Flake-o. Then he put his hands up to his mouth and leaned his head back like he was taking a drink.

All of them savages started jumping around and saying, "Flu Flu Flake-o."

I punched Lord Jesus and asked him, "What in tarnation does Flu Flu Flake-o mean?"

He give me a dirty look like I had spawned right out of hell and muttered at me: "Keep yore mouth shut. You gonna have yore head up on a pole before I can save you." Then he hollered loud as he could: *"Flu Flu Flake-o!"*

All of a sudden Lord Jesus cut out away from me, right through the crowd, and Oli-Oli taken off behind him. Oli-Oli had a hard time keeping up because he was so old, but Lord Jesus looked back over his shoulder and seen this and cut down a little. Right behind Oli-Oli and Lord Jesus the rest of them converted savages went single file.

It was a sight. I didn't even think to myself: Right here is your chance, Rover Youngblood, to turn on your heels and get back to your mare Bessie and take to the road before your head is cut off and set on a stick. I didn't think of nothing but what I was looking at: Lord Jesus in front in his long underwear with his black stringy hair flying in all directions and right behind him Oli-Oli neckid but for his turkey feathers and trying to keep up and behind him the men, women, and younguns, some neckid and some not, chasing after. They was

35

all yelling, "Flu Flu Flake-o!" Lord Jesus would lead them up one path lined with fruit jars and down another and up one and down another. Lord Jesus started slapping his rump with his hands and all of them would do that. Then he stuck out his left arm to the side, and they did. Then the right arm.

I was reminded of this here game that my brother Ed and brother Silas and me use to play when we was little where the one in front done something and the ones in back that was following had to do it too. I always got to be the one in front because I was the oldest.

Lord Jesus come to the main house and stopped. He was sweating and panting something awful, and so was all of them. Oli-Oli just sunk down to the ground and leaned his head against the house. They all went down.

It seemed like a long time before any of them said anything or even moved much except for panting. I wasn't surprised the first one to get over it was Lord Jesus. He raised up his head a little bit because it had been hung down like he was praying. He raised it up some more and looked out over his congregation. His eyes come on out to me standing there and he jerked up like he'd forgot all about me.

He put his hands up to his mouth to make a funnel and yelled at me: *"Unclean, unsaved, manure of the stables and barns, bearer of false witnesses, dirt of the womb, and all that's unholy!"*

He stopped and waited. I put my hands in my pockets and didn't know what to do.

"O killer of innocent children, O soothsayer!"

All this was to me, but I hadn't killed no innocent children or otherwise and I didn't know what a soothsayer was. I thought to myself he'd unravel it all after a while.

"You hear me?"

I taken my hands out of my pockets and said, "Yessir."

"O fornicator, come forward unto me!"

I didn't move because I didn't know if he was through or not.

"You hear me? Come here!"

I moved along fast as I could not running and made my way through the stretched-out congregation till I got up to the Lord Jesus Turner. He was still setting down.

He looked up with them mean snake eyes and mumbled to me, "Cross your heart and hope to die and hope your old mammy will die too, if you got a mammy, that here on out you'll rid yourself of the tarnish of the flesh."

It seemed like it was the best thing to do to cross my heart, so I did.

"Say, I hope to die," the Lord Jesus said.

"Hope to die."

"And hope my old mammy dies."

"And hope my old mammy dies." But I said to myself, I don't hope neither one of us dies now or evermore.

"If I don't rid my rotten flesh of the tarnish."

I said that after him.

All them converted savages had been looking at me like I was a oddity pulled out of a well. Especially Oli-Oli, setting right there beside Lord Jesus. He had little cuts for eyes you couldn't hardly see in that wrinkled face about the size of my two fists put together. He was taking me all in, though. I could tell it. He had his

37

head leaned back and his hands was holding to his privates.

Lord Jesus jumped up and said top of his voice, *"Flu Flu Flake-o!"* so loud I near about wet myself. He jumped over one and another of his congregation till he got inside the door of the main house. Oli-Oli went next. Then they all went.

I stood at the door and taken in the bottom floor of the main house. Like I said, this house like the other houses was made out of old Vicks Salve and Nehi and Royal Crown Cola and other such signs, and now and then would be a big gap. It was that way, and the floor was dirt with dried-out pine needles strewed on it. Directly ahead of me, the other side of the room, they was two sawhorses with planks laid across them and on top of these they was two cane-bottom chairs. In front of the chairs and on the ground was another cane-bottom chair. Up above all this was a tin sign, red painted on white: LORD JESUS TURNER, VIRGIN MARY TURNER, OLI-OLI MESNGR. BOY. Going from the sign on either side over to the corners was strings of tin cans. Right to the left of the platform was a table with thirty-forty bottles of what I taken to be homebrew. It looked like everything was got up for a party except for the bones and what the sign said. The walls to either side, to my right and left, was covered with tree branches of ever description, some of them dried out and some of them fresh.

I mean it was hot in there. All I was was at the door but the heat swum up and hit you.

The congregation was taking their places on the floor and most of them setting cross-legged. Oli-Oli set down on the chair in front of the platform. Lord Jesus was already up there on the platform, his legs spraddled, and he had his long underwear unbuttoned down to about his belly button. He looked awful hot after that running and now this oven.

Everbody got just as quiet, and the Lord Jesus Turner closed his eyes and stretched both arms out in front of him. His hands was fists. It sounded like he said: "You boo bit you." But he said it fast and all together. Then ever one of them converted savages started saying, "You boo bit you," but they didn't say it all of them at the same time. They just said it whenever they taken a notion to. It made a odd-sounding noise.

Lord Jesus leaned over and punched Oli-Oli on the head. Oli-Oli seemed to know what the sign was because he went straight over to the table with the bottles on it and got one and brought it to Lord Jesus.

Lord Jesus Turner held up his right hand, palm forward, said, "You boo bit you" one more time, and everbody got quiet again. One baby youngun started bawling and Lord Jesus kept holding up his hand till its mammy or somebody got it shut up.

All quiet and he taken a long swaller from the bottle, then made a sound like "Ahhhhhh" that come through his nose.

"In the name of Number One who is Me," he said.

He taken another snort.

"Number Two who is Me."

One more snort and he called off Number Three who was him too. He followed that up with "You boo bit you" and right then was the sign for Oli-Oli to start passing out bottles to the congregation. Everbody was taking a snort including the younguns. Oli-Oli set back

39

down in his chair and started pulling on his own bottle. The way they was all going after it I could see we would have us some drunk converted savages right soon.

They wasn't a bottle for everbody, just a bottle for ever third-fourth one, and they would pass it to one another. None of the younguns had a bottle to itself.

They started making some racket but it was low and I couldn't tell what they said. Some of the women would giggle and some of the men laugh but not loud yet, still low, so by the racket they made, if you didn't look at what you seen, it could of been a church social that me and my folks went to back at Clearpoint.

It wasn't long, though, till they started getting louder and I knowed they was getting high. Lord Jesus must of saw this because he stood up and holding the bottle to his side said, "Mothas mothas."

Oli-Oli stood up too and said, "Mothas mothas." They all joined in but stayed setting down.

In the middle of that, Lord Jesus come out louder than I'd ever heared him—probably because of the homebrew—and pointed at me and said: *"Dung of the sheep and ruination, breeder of wars and rumors of wars."*

He let it go at that but kept holding out his finger at me. Ever one of them converted savages turned around to look at me, all of them quiet, and I said to myself, Rover Youngblood, this don't look good because in about two minutes you may be a sacrifice with your head chopped off and put on a stick and circulated among the homebrew.

It seemed like Lord Jesus held his pose for ten minutes

or more but it wasn't that long. He broke it off by telling me: "Come on up here and let me look at your eyes to see if you've shed any taint. Don't want the holy homebrew ruint."

I made my way over the black arms and legs of the congregation with Lord Jesus talking right on and saying it when I got up to him: "I can tell by his eyes and by his teeth and by the way his hair stands if he is fit for Heaven. I can tell by the way his feet is planted on God's good earth that is mine because I am the One, the Two, and the Three."

I was right in front of him, about two inches from touching Oli-Oli.

"Look up at me," Lord Jesus said.

I did, and I didn't like the way he looked. If he looked ugly without homebrew he looked like a haint with homebrew in him. Them side teeth missing and them sharp other teeth and the hair hanging down the sides of his face. I don't mind if I say I was ascared.

"Open up that mouth so's I can look at them teeth. So's I can inspect them for purity."

I did. He leaned down close and looked and said, "Naw. Naw. They is each and ever one a separate devil. Naw."

I shut my mouth and he said, "Lean down yore head so's I can see how the hair stands."

I did that and he said "Naw" again.

"You reckin me and Oli-Oli and all of these sanctified savages who has spent money not to mention time and effort is goin to let you who is unclean and not fit for nothin but hell stand here and take the blessing off of this here homebrew?"

41

I didn't say nothing.

"Do you reckin?"

"I don't reckin so," I told him. I didn't know what else to tell him. It looked like if I said Yes or No or Go to Hell it was about the same thing, which was off comes my head.

"The way you reckin is this, you reckin right."

Lord Jesus Turner was bent towards me again.

"I'm gonna make you clean," he said and set back in his chair, straight, like that was that.

I started to ask myself how he was gonna do it but I told myself, Just wait and see.

He told me: "Get up here on this platform and stand beside me and face the congregation."

"Thief among whores," he said, "I want you to stand here before this fine congregation of sanctified Africans and confess ever black and bloody sin that comes to mind that you have ever did."

He said to them and they said after him: "Dreama dreama dreama."

I thought to myself that he was getting his car into all of this and sure enough he was. He told the audience: "I have got a automobile, name of Dreama Glory, that has got winders to go up and down by the button, that can take itself apart by removin its top, that can make loud and joyful music unto me who is the Lord Jesus, and it is made out of *tin and metal*. *It* has not sinned. *It* does not have to confess. But this one *here*"—and he give me a hard punch in the ribs with his finger—"has got to confess before one and all before he can even be in the same class as the Dreama Glory."

They all hollered, "Dreama dreama dreama."

"Pull down yore overalls," Lord Jesus Turner said right quick.

I turned around to look at him like I didn't know what he meant, and I didn't.

"Pull down yore overalls for all the crowd to look at yore shame out of the Garden of Eden while you tell them about yore sins."

I thought, I don't care none to do this with all them women setting out there even if they do come out of Africa. I don't care to stand up neckid in front of no congregation, white, black, men, women, younguns, or what. Besides that, I ain't got no underwear on.

"Drop them overalls."

I unbuckled the galluses and looked straight ahead at the wall the other side of the room. Then I dropped the galluses and down went the overalls. There I was neckid from the waist down.

The Lord Jesus inspected me and said, "You have swam in the pits of Jezebel."

My overalls was around my feet, so I couldn't move my feet much if I wanted to. I held my hands down straight at the side.

"Start to confessin, and don't leave out nothin, including rape, murder, jackin off, cohabitation, robbery, and mean thoughts."

I thought of Shady Grove Church and that time ma had made me go down front to confess before the preacher. That time I got away with telling that I'd smoked rabbit tobacco and said cuss words. I knew the Lord Jesus Turner wasn't going to put up with no such confession as that.

"Well," I said and I was still looking right straight at

43

the wall, "they was this one time when me and my two brothers, name of Ed and Silas Youngblood, we was goin possum hunting in the woods down back of where I live near Clearpoint and as we was goin through the woods we come onto this little house that looked like it didn't have nobody in it, so I knocked on the door and didn't nobody come. And so me and Silas and Ed all went in and looked all around the house and so when we come to the bed here was this baby on it, about a foot long, it was a girl baby that had curly hair, and so she looked up at me and smiled three-four times, and I said, 'Baby, don't smile at me.' She started to cry and I told her to hush up her mouth. Well, she didn't but kept up bawling, so I said to my brother Silas, 'Silas, hand me that ax that is standin over there by the fireplace because I am goin to cut this purty baby's head off and take it on home with me.' Well, Silas and Ed both tried to get me not to do it because they said it was sinful and that God wouldn't like it but I said, 'I don't care one bit,' and then I said the Lord's name in vain three-four times."

I rested for a minute and looked down at the congregation for the first time. They was all setting still as could be, except for taking swigs off of their bottles, and the way they was looking at me it seemed like they knowed what I was saying. Maybe they all knowed two languages or something.

I went on: "I taken that ax and cut off her head with one stroke as clean as if you'd took a razor to that purty baby girl. Blood went flyin everwhere. I was soakin in it from head to foot and I liked it. I picked up the baby girl's head by the hair an started swingin it around and I said to Ed and Silas, 'Don't try to stop me at nothin

44

because I'll knock you down with this here baby's head.'
They didn't try to stop me but both got down and started
prayin for my soul. I blasphemed the Lord and taken
the baby's head on home with me and throwed it in the
fireplace and watched it burn."

I stopped and waited.

Finally Lord Jesus said, "Amen. Dreama dreama."

Oli-Oli said, "Amen. Dreama dreama." And the
others did too.

Lord Jesus leaned back to look up at me, taken a swig,
and said, "Go on with yore confessin. You got yoreself
a half a inch closer to Heaven. Verily verily I say unto
you in my name."

Oli-Oli had been setting with his back to me but now
he turned around so he could look up and listen.

"Well, back at Clearpoint, the other side of it, north-
west of it, they was this nice old lady with gray hair who
had not ever did harm to as much as a fly and she had
this beautiful granddaughter with black curly hair who
prayed and went to church all the time with her grandmother. I'd been thinkin about the young gal. Havin
all kind of bad thoughts about her. Ever night I would
lay in bed and think bad thoughts, till one night I
jumped up out of bed neckid as when I was sprung from
the womb and I grabbed my shotgun and went tearin
out to rape this girl by the name of Erleen Dawsie
Baldingham. Her mammy and pappy was dead and she
was just a orphan who chopped cotton to keep bread and
water in the mouth of her grandmother. She was so beautiful your eyes would fall out of your head if you looked
at her too long.

"I went walking neckid right through Clearpoint and

some old man that was settin there in front of Driver's Hardware Store by the moonlight and that ought to of been in bed hollered out at me, 'Boy, what are you doin runnin around neckid on the streets of the town? I am a good Christian and I ain't use to puttin up with sech as this.' I cussed and blowed his head off with my shotgun, then went right on till I got to the house of this here gal and her old grandmother. It was quiet as could be and they had a nice yard that they had took care of, the old grandmother always sweepin it up and settin out flowers in car tires and a nice vegetable garden out in back with fresh tomatoes and okra, while this beautiful young gal that had these beautiful bosoms was out choppin cotton and gettin blisters on her white hands.

"I peeped in the window and seen them layin in their separate beds, the old grandmother snoring a little bit but calm and restful lookin. The gal was layin on the bed without a stitch of nothin on her. She didn't have but one nightgown and she had washed it out but it hadn't dried yet. I went stormin into the house as wild as a animal. The old grandmother looked up and seen me neckid with my shotgun. She started to scream and call on God, and I said, 'You scream one more time, you old scarecrow, and I'll blow your head off.' She did and I did. It was a mess. They wasn't a sign left of her head except for a few gray hairs with some blood on them."

Then he said, "Take some of this here homebrew to help you with yore salvation, name of me." He handed me the bottle and I taken a swaller. I nearly strangled and it didn't set good on my stomach. I hadn't had nothin to eat all day. It didn't look like I would, even if

I was alive to, if I had to go confessing to all the sins knowed to man.

Lord Jesus pushed the bottle back at me. "Take some more. It's holy." I did and it wasn't long till I could feel it.

"Git back to yore sins," Lord Jesus said.

"When the old grandmother was dead I looked over at the beautiful young gal that was laying on the bed and tremblin and cryin, like she knowed what was goin on in my head. She was right and I started towards her makin a growlin sound in my throat. She hollered out in a pitiful voice, 'Don't tech me, don't tech me,' but I cussed and said, 'What do you think I'm doin here neckid for in the middle of the night? I ain't only goin to tech you, I'm goin to rape you even if you are a virgin and a orphan that has worked her hand to the bone all of her life. Look at your grandmother there in a puddle of blood. She warn't but a old scarecrow even if she was a Christian. Furthermore, I ain't got no use for Christians or the likes of them. I am going to rape you and I don't want you to say a word. Do you hear me?'

"She nodded her head up and down with these pitiful tears runnin down. I stood there lookin at her beautiful neckid body and I got excited. I jumped on top of her and raped her five times. I was about played out so I said to her, 'Wait till I get back my strenth and I will rape you some more. If you say a word to me I'll blow off your head with this here shotgun.'

"She didn't say nothin, so after a while I raped her some more. On about morning we was layin there in bed together and I said, 'Honey, how would you like to be a whore for me? We could make lots of money and I

47

could buy you some purty clothes from Birmingham, them flashy ones like whores wear, and you could paint your face.' She studied about it for a little while and said that since she was ruint she might as well go along and make the most of it, that I had drug her down to the flamin pits of hell and she was beginnin to like it.

"In the next week I went out over the country and raped a bunch of other virgin gals, red-headed, black-headed, blond, ever one of them a doozie as to looks and the body, and I brought them all back to this old grand-mother's house to join this other gal that I had raped first. They was all glad to be there and got all painted up and went runnin around neckid. I'd service each one of them ever night before I went to sleep.

"Finally I said, 'We ain't makin no money like this here. I want you gals to go out and round up the pore innocent farm boys that has saved their money and bring them back here and charge them a dollar a throw.'

"Well, they did, and taken in about five hunnert dollars. I got tired of them and shot ever last one. I reckin they're all in hell now. I run off to Birmingham."

Lord Jesus looked up at me like he didn't much take to the end of my confession. I knowed it speeded up too much but I was getting tired of them particular sins. It seemed like they was going to have to be the same thing over and over.

Them savages hadn't let out a sound up till now. All of a sudden they started clapping their hands, I reckin at the confession I'd made. Oli-Oli was clapping too.

Lord Jesus was looking wall-eyed at me. I could tell he was feeling the homebrew.

"Boy," he said and it sounded like he had cornmeal

batter in his mouth, "it takes mighteous forgivin on my part to forgive that kind of a sin, but I am capable. I have got the power in me. I am the One and the Two and the Three. Take some more of this here homebrew which is certain speed on yore highway to forgiveness."

I didn't want to but I did. What I wanted was something to eat. And to cool off.

Lord Jesus hollered, "Dreama dreama," without much spirit to it. All of them others answered him back with a lots of spirit. They didn't stop with Dreama dreama. They went on and on. They was happy.

"Boy," Lord Jesus said to me, and that's all he got out of his mouth. He fell right out of the chair and off the platform and flat as a flitter on his face to the ground. He nearly hit Oli-Oli.

It must have been some kind of a sign, because Oli-Oli climbed up on the platform and set down in the Lord Jesus Turner's chair. All the other savages started jumping up and whooping. It wasn't no time till they was pure commotion in that room, with man, woman, and youngun jumping and jigging and letting out squealing sounds and hollers.

Oli-Oli motioned for me to set down in the chair next to him. I pulled up my overalls and set down and just watched the dancing for a while. Lord Jesus Turner was still laying there with his face in the dirt, and it looked like he might be there for a long time. They wasn't anybody paying no attention. If any of them dancers come up around him they just jumped over and went right on.

Oli-Oli pulled his chair over close to me and said with his hand up to his mouth so's I could hear: "Them niggers is havin them a *good* time. Holy watta is runnin through 'em. They is all my fambly and ever one saved."

He smiled like he was mighty proud. I couldn't get over it that he could talk American.

"Where did you learn the unknown tongue?" I asked him.

He looked at me like he didn't know what I was talking about.

"Dat gal yonder is my wife." He pointed to a gal that looked to be twenty-thirty year old and didn't have nothing on but a red and white polka dot cloth at her privates.

"She my granddaughta too," he said.

I thought: You all have younguns and they'll grow up to be crazy as betsy bugs.

Oli-Oli started giggling and pointed for me to see. A man and woman started playing leap frog and right soon everbody started playing leap frog, including the younguns. It looked like a good time was being had by all. I wondered to myself what the Lord Jesus would think about it, if it was Christian or not.

"Where do you come from, Oli-Oli?" I asked him.

He looked at me and then studied some and looked off and then looked back at me. I could just barely see them little eyes.

"I come from *God*. I swum the air of heben, I flown like a bird, I perched in the belly of my mammy, and I struck on this earth."

I meant where did he use to live, near what town, but didn't look like I'd ever be able to get something like that out of him.

"You been saved?" Oli-Oli said.

I told him right quick that I had shore been saved.

He nodded and seemed to be satisfied.

It looked like right here while the Lord Jesus was laying asleep and everbody was having such a good time might be when I ought to get out of there. I never had watered my mare Bessie and that was on my mind.

I leaned so Oli-Oli could hear me. "Oli-Oli, I'm gonna have to go but I thank you for showin me a good time. You have got a nice family and a purty wife. I've got this here mare name of Bessie that ain't had water all day and me and her made a long trip this morning. And I haven't eat nothin yet. So's I'm gonna go on and see about my mare and maybe I can come back and visit with you sometime.

All he done was nod, didn't call out the law or nothing, and then he shook my hand and said, "Dreama dreama dreama."

I said, "Dreama dreama dreama," and then I got down off of the platform and made my way the best I could through all of them converted savages playing leap frog.

It was a sight cooler the minute I got out of that room.

Chapter 7

I GOT BACK to the barn and there was Bessie just as happy as you please, in a stall next to the Lord Jesus' fancy car. I said, "Bessie, honey, they is things on this earth that you have not saw yet and I am goin to do my best to keep your eyes lookin the other way. And don't ever get to be a Christian, even if the Lord Jesus Turner did say your eyes is set good and you're free from sin. You wouldn't know what was happenin to you if you was to be a Christian, Bessie, and if you was to backslide they might be somebody would cut off your head and put it on a stick."

I patted her on the flank.

"You wait right here and I'll get you some cool well water."

When I was drawing from the well I heard somebody

say from behind the back screen door, "Whur's the Lord Jesus at?"

I shaded my eyes and still couldn't see nobody. I knowed it was the Virgin Mary though.

"He's down yonder with the savages at their meetin house."

"They is chulrun who was saved by the Lord Jesus my son, without cohabitation."

"Yes, ma'am. He's with the converted savages and Oli-Oli. Everbody's havin a good time."

"Is the Lord Jesus drunk on the holy water?"

"Yes, ma'am, he is laying on his face in the dirt."

It was a few minutes before she said anything.

"Come on in here and let me look at you. I'll cook up somethin for you to eat."

I told her I had to go and water Bessie first and then I'd come on in.

"Hurry up because it's hot in here with this stove agoin."

"Yes, ma'am," and I watered Bessie as fast as I could and told her we'd be leaving that place as soon as I could see my way to it.

I knocked at the screen door and the Virgin unlatched it. There she stood in front of me, all six and a half foot and still wearing her civilian clothes that was black and down to the floor. She'd pulled her long hair around so it hung down both sides on the front. The Virgin hadn't got no purtier since I had last saw her. She motioned for me to set down at this table that had a oilcloth tablecloth on it of pink and blue flowers where they wasn't scrubbed away.

53

The room wasn't no size at all, with a wood stove in it going full for hell so's it made this room hotter'n the one I just left. They was a cupboard, a electric icebox that was awful dirty, two crates to set on at the table, a picture took from a magazine and wrote on it: Best wishes, from Lana Turner, a picture of the Virgin and the Lord Jesus setting in their car Dreama and both of them with smiles so big you could see where the Lord Jesus' teeth was missing, a poem tore out from a newspaper:

> When you're in the valley know
> Christ beside your side will go.
> Do not have a single care,
> Jesus Christ is everywhere.
> When you all the rivers leap
> Don't think Christ will be asleep.
> High and low and through the air
> Jesus Christ is everywhere.

(and I thought to myself, ma would like that poem), a nail with a red bead necklace hung on it, and a little pasteboard sign that said in ink: UP! UP! EVER UP!

I set down on one of the crates. The Virgin was at the stove frying meat and muttering something to herself that I couldn't understand.

In a little bit she said, "You didn't bring no blessed homebrew back with you?"

I told her I didn't.

Then she said, "Constipation!"

"Ma'am," I said.

"Constipation! Constipation! It's worse thataway.

Here!" And she stuck a plate in front of me with two pork chops, grits with pork chop grease, and two hunks of cold corn bread. My belly was moaning and crying for it, and I taken up the fork that was laying there and started to haul in.

The Virgin said, "Wait! I got to get something, for one thing, and besides we ain't had prayer. They ain't nothing eat or drank in this house but what me or the Lord Jesus Turner has got to bless it first. I'll be right back."

She wasn't gone no time till she come back with a bottle of homebrew. She set down on the other crate and poured her some homebrew in a jelly glass. Then she poured me some in another one. I didn't care for none of it but knowed I would have to be polite and join in with her.

The Virgin Mary said, "This here has done been blessed down yonder where them niggers is at, so you can go ahead and drink it. Go ahead. It's good for you and will wash out your soul."

She drunk hers down in one long swaller and then set there and waited for me to drink mine. I did, but it taken me more than one swaller and I about near throwed up.

"I'll say the prayer, so keep your head down and your eyes shet tight," the Virgin said.

By time my eyes was shut she'd started off: "I pray to myself and to the Lord Jesus, who is down yonder with them niggers drunk on his own blessing: I thank you for giving to yourself what you have gave and to the bounty that you out of the goodness of your heart have gave to everybody else includin this youngun settin here that's off on his way to the big highway through life before he comes to the end of the road whar the cars can't go no further and they is a sign that reads, THIS HERE IS THE END OF THE LINE AND YORE BODY WILL TURN TO ASHES AND THE WORMS WILL EAT IT UP. I want to say I thank you, you who is unspoiled, untainted, and has not knowed the touch of man or his craving desires and who ain't tasted the mangy fruit off of that blighted tree of Eden—I want to thank you yourself for the hog meat set here before this boy, this corn pone, these here grits, and the clothes we wear upon our backs. Name of me and the Lord Jesus. Amen."

I looked up and she said, "Dig in."

It don't take much of a cook to fry pork chops because you just fry them till they get done. I have did it myself. But them pork chops set before me by the Virgin tasted as good as any my ma had ever cooked, and the corn bread wasn't bad. It needed a little something in it or something took out, but it wasn't bad.

The Virgin had her squared-off chin cupped in her hands and was watching me eat. I didn't notice it at first, I was eating so hard, and then when I did I wished she'd look off somewhere else.

"How much poontang you had?" the Virgin asked me. She didn't say poontang, but something else.

I don't know if I got red or not but I felt red and didn't say nothing.

"Give me a rough estimate. It won't be a lie if you get it wrong."

"Four-five times," I said. "I don't know."

"Constipation."

I never had figured out what she meant by that, and

I didn't know now, or as to whether it was good or bad or what.

"They is chulrun out of Israel that give faith to a golden calf. I seen 'em myself."

"Yes, ma'am." I was finishing up my last bite of corn-bread.

When she wasn't setting there looking right straight at me, her eyes would be off somewhere like they wasn't looking at nothing and it was scary because of how her eyes was set back in her head and dark all around them.

"It was one time that me and Tunis, back home before I met up with the Lord Jesus, was givin a tent show down at Ardmore. Tunis was my earthly husband and come from Crosspoint, Mississippi, and has not been reborn last time I heard but jined up with a travelin carnival owned by the Addison Brothers and fed chickens to alkyholics. I said to Tunis, 'You ain't doin nothin but throwin away yore life runnin after ever no-count woman, livin in show business, which'll drop you as quick as it'll look at you, and you gettin up in years, they won't be the young gals to give you money after while. Come on and be a disciple of me and the Lord Jesus.' That 'ere Tunis wouldn't listen."

She waited a minute and was looking way off some-wheres. I had my eye to the stove to see if it was anything left to eat.

"They was many a night before I got to be a Virgin that I had earthly paradise with Tunis, who was a man that knowed his way. I'd say, 'Tunis, what did they do with you when you was a baby, to keep you in control?' and Tunis would say they couldn't do nothin with him but lock up all the gal babies.

"So I met the Lord Jesus Turner and got to be the Virgin Mary and ever since then me and him and others has had to have cohabitation by symbols.

"I have longed after Tunis and the mortal guise and I hereby forgive myself. Name of me and Lord Jesus Turner. Amen."

They didn't seem to be anything else to eat, not that I could see.

The Virgin jumped up from the table and held out her dress to the sides. "Ain't it a purty getup. If it's anything I like it's clothes. After a while I'll show you what I wear in the Shrine of the Holiness and what I've got for party wear which ain't the same as civilian."

She must of forgot I had seen her Holiness dress.

"It is shore a purty dress, ma'am. Ain't it hot on you in here, with it reachin to the floor and long sleeves?"

"I ain't never sweat in my life," she said, like I had said something ugly to her and she was mad.

I wondered what it was that happened at the tent show down at Ardmore, when her and Tunis was going together. She had got off the track or decided not to tell me, one of the two, so I up and asked her.

A odd look come on her face and her eyes went off somewheres. "I was doin this Dance of the Veils and was called Ulanda the Lady from the Unknown Kingdom. It was a act enjoyed by all, who was men and boys because women was not allowed. We had us a tent and Tunis would stand there and explain all I had went through in the ways of the body and all that had befell me in the hands of apes and gorillas and missionaries and sech. Then I would give interpatations. I had a sight

58

of costumes. Gold and silver and fringes and the like.

"And then up come the Lord Jesus Turner one night to see my act and afterwards back of the tent told me how good I had did and that when he seen me do the fight with the Congo ape to save my chastity he knowed it was wrote in Heaven that I was to be the Virgin Mary who was his own mother.

"He taken from his pocket this here nail that is yonder in the Shrine of the Holiness and held it out in the palm of his hand and said to me, 'This here nail is one that was drove through my hand when I got crucified, and if you don't believe me look at the scar I got.' I looked and shore enough they was a scar, and they was a scar in his other hand too. He said, 'Take a hold of this nail fer a minute and notice how yore spirit will be improved and notice how you'll have the strenth to go on no matter how deep in sorrow you might ever be.' I taken a hold and it was like he said. Right then and there I turned into a virgin. I told Tunis he'd have to find him somebody else to be Ulanda from the Unknown Kingdom, and I went packin with the Lord Jesus Turner."

"Has that there nail got blood on it?" I asked her.

"Yessir, it has got the Lord Jesus Turner's blood on it and it is rusty to boot."

I was getting ready to ask her if I could be excused, so I could get Bessie and we would be on our way before it started getting dark. But I wanted to see that nail and I wanted to see the Shrine of the Holiness too. A opportunity like this didn't come up ever time you turned around. I figured Manfred City would wait on me and not walk off.

"You reckin I could see that there nail? I wouldn't have to tech it."

She leaned across the table, put her chin back in her hands and studied me. She blinked her eyes and frowned.

"The Lord Jesus would be agin it, but he's drunk and wouldn't know it except fer the fact that he knows even to the last sparrow that falls from the air. I might show you and I might not. You never can tell. He is my own son, so it looks like he oughta do like I say sometimes and have some respect for his mammy. It says that in the Bible, which he wrote, to have respect fer yore mammy and pappy."

I told her it did, because I knowed that much about the Bible.

"Come on in the settin room and be comforble. I wanta show you some stuff."

She opened a door to a hallway that was dark and when we was going through it she turned around and said, "You're cute." Then she pinched me on the chest and went on. She didn't wait for me to give her no answer. We come into the room where I'd first met the Lord Jesus.

"Set down over there and won't be no time atall till I'm back and got a big surprise fer you."

She went into the Shrine of the Holiness trying to wiggle her hips but not doing much of a job at it. I knowed she was playing up on sex and it didn't seem right, with her being the Virgin Mary.

I set down in the deep chair and wondered what brother Ed and brother Silas was doing and if ma was grieving over me and praying to the Lord Jesus Turner or any other Lord Jesus for me to come on back home and if pa was sorry he tried to give me a beating. I was thinking that maybe I ought to not of run off and maybe me and Bessie would hike it back to Clearpoint, because things was straighter back at home and not in such a muddle as they was here, and if they was this way here, not no further than what we was from home, what was it gonna be ten mile on down and then twenty mile and then at Manfred City? Good times come to my head: looking for rattlers with my brothers, having ma's fried chicken and biscuits for breakfast, loving Sandra Jean— and that's what done it, Sandra Jean, that's what made me decide to keep right on going, her and that baby that like as not had Jimmy Lunsford for a daddy. Yessir, I'd keep on going.

Chapter 8

"THIS HERE IS A PARTY DRESS," the Virgin said and kind of skipped out into the room, but more like a mule than a woman.

I had never saw such a getup, including the Virgin's civilian clothes and her Shrine of the Holiness clothes. These would of put you in mind of being somewhere you wasn't suppose to be. They was a red skirt that come down to the floor and looked like it had about eighty yard of cloth in it because it had all these here folds and pleats, and tacked on to the bottom of it was hearts cut out of white. Up above she had on something like a blouse, I don't know what you'd call it, but it was black and of a netlike material so's you could see through it, right at her bosoms. She'd got her hair piled up on top of her head and they was two peacock feathers stuck in it, blowing to the breeze. On both arms she had four-five bracelets each, and all different colors and made out of different things. Last was her face that she had painted up: it was blue all around her eyes where they was normally black, she'd painted her lips red and pulled them out longer than they ought to be, and on each cheek she had a red spot about the size of a silver dollar.

"My name is Ava Maureen," she said in a prissy-sounding voice and put her hands on her hips and then behind her head and then shook herself.

"I ain't never *heared* of the Virgin Mary Turner, wouldn't know who she was if I was to see her, and I come from Birmingham, Alabama, in the part whur the rich folks lives and I have traveled considerable to Mobile and Montgomery."

She walked up to me and took me by the hair and held my head back. "You're right cute yourself, if I do say so. What's yore name?"

I had already told my name and she knowed it as well as I did. As to her being Ava Maureen, I didn't know what she was talking about, as well as she hadn't never heard of the Virgin Mary Turner.

To get her to turn aloose of my hair I figured I'd better tell her a name.

"My name is O. T. Jenkins the Third."

"That's a cute name," she said and whirled around. "Whur do you come from exactly?"

"I come from New York City, whur I was raised up of foreign parentage."

"I swan," she said and giggled. "I'm gonna set down and talk to you a while and see what all we has in common."

She pulled up a cane-bottom chair from beside the

63

fireplace and set down right in front of me so that our legs was touching.

"Do you like my outfit?" she said but didn't give me time to answer. "I bought this here at Heinman's in Birmingham and it cost a sight of money. Money ain't no problem to me. Looka here." She fished out from her waist a ten-dollar bill and handed it to me. "Put that in yore pocket and have a big time. Money ain't no object."

I thanked her and hoisted my rear end up a little to put the money in my pocket.

"Do you like this here top part?" She run her hands down over her bosoms.

I taken a quick look. Her bosoms hung down like they was wet paper sacks.

"Yes, ma'am," I told her. "The whole getup looks mighty nice."

"I knowed you'd like it."

She kept this here grin on her face that didn't look like it would go away.

"You visitin here, Ava Maureen?" I thought I might as well go on with her and let her be whoever she said she was.

"I'm passin through," she said, "thinkin of buyin up some land. I'm thinkin of buildin a factry. Then I'm goin on to Hollywood because they want me to be in the movies.

"And what do *you* do?" she said.

She put her hand on my leg and rubbed on it.

"I'm in the mule tradin business," I said, "but my office is in one of them buildings in New York City. I'm just passin through myself. I'm lookin fer mules."

"I swan."

64

Her hand was still laying there on my leg and I could tell what she was up to. Whatever her name was, she wasn't what I was looking for. I took up her hand and played with it a little while and then dropped it down on her lap.

"I use to teach school before I went into show business. At a college. Ain't no tellin how many books I've read."

"What was they about?"

She still had her hand in her lap.

"Varus things. Some was about love."

"I ain't never read any books, because the mule trade keeps me so busy."

"You ever read *True Romances*?"

"No, ma'am, it's my wife that does all the readin. She reads about everthing in sight. Me and her's got eight younguns and she's jealous of ever woman I look at. She follows me around and she's done shot four-five women. Like as not she's hidin out around here somewheres."

I thought maybe that would put a little worry in Ava Maureen's head but it didn't. Next thing I knowed she was off of her chair and setting on top of me in the deep chair. I couldn't move or hardly breathe.

She started putting her hands all over me and down inside of my overalls.

"I seen my wife lookin in at the door!" I told her.

"Hesh up!" She'd got my galluses unbuckled by now and was pulling off the buttons of my shirt.

"I'm the Lord Jesus Christ!" I hollered and give her a push as hard as I could. All six and a half foot of Ava Maureen hit the floor and it made the whole room shake. I was standing up trying to buckle my galluses and she was reaching over trying to pull my pants down.

"The Lord Jesus Turner is acoming! I can see him out of the winder!"

"Constipation!" she hollered and jumped up and taken about three long hops to the Shrine of the Holiness. She banged the door shut.

I had made it up about seeing the Lord Jesus Turner. It seemed like it was the best way to get Ava Maureen Virgin Mary off of me. I had never thought I would have to turn a woman down but a woman like this here one had not ever come to me even in bad dreams.

I got myself together and was planning to go right out the back way to get Bessie. Then we'd hike it.

I was at the hall when I heard the Virgin slam the door. She had on her civilian dress, and she'd like as not pulled it right on top of the other one. They hadn't been enough time for her to change. Her hair was hanging down, but she still had the paint on her face.

"Whur you off to?" she said.

"I was gonna hitch Bessie out whur she could get some grass."

"Whur's the Lord Jesus Turner at?"

"He started comin this way and then he turned around and when back whur he come from."

"Whur did Ava Maureen go to?"

I told her I didn't know that. I hadn't never met nobody by the name of Ava Maureen.

I was still standing at the door to the hall and I said: "Virgin, I'm gonna have to be on my way because it won't be too long till the sun starts goin down and I've got me a long ways to go. I thank you fer cookin me up them pork chops and grits and lettin me drink the homebrew that was blessed. You tell the Lord Jesus Turner good-bye fer me and you and him be good and take care of yourselves."

I put out my hand to shake with her but she didn't move to take it.

"Just fer that," she said, "you ain't gonna get to see the Shrine of the Holiness."

Then the Virgin stuck out her tongue at me.

All I wanted to do was get out of there. I didn't care if I seen any Shrine of the Holiness or not.

"Maybe I can come by and see it some other time," I told her.

"Won't be no other time. Armygeddon will be here before you know it. You and all that's like you will be roastin and spitten and poppin in hell."

"Yes, ma'am," I said and turned to go.

"Wait! I got somethin fer you."

She went into the Shrine of the Holiness for about two minutes and was back.

"Here," she said, "hold out yore hand."

I did and she gave me a rusty nail.

"That there is the Lord Jesus', that generates his power. Take it and you might be saved. You might come to be Lord Jesus Youngblood."

I told her thank you.

Chapter 9

ME AND BESSIE was down the road about two mile and I said, "Bessie, honey, when we get on down the way some and I spot woods, I'll stop and let you graze. We're too close to the Lord Jesus and the Virgin Mary to stop now. When he sobers up and finds out I got his nail that is his generatin power they ain't no tellin what he might do. Would he become a everday man or the Lord Jesus without generatin power or the devil or what? He'd be mad, anyhow. He has got a bad temper and I'd as soon stay shut of him.

"And, Bessie, looka here, if he ain't got that 'ere nail he might not be saved no more, and if he ain't saved, why, them converted savages might can tell it by his teeth and the way his hair stands and the way his feet is planted on the ground. They might cut his head off and put it on a stick. I wouldn't want him to get kilt, but if they was to start out after him it might make him have some feelin for other folks.

"As far as I can tell, the Virgin is the Virgin whenever she wants to be. So I reckin she ain't got nothin to worry about. If the Lord Jesus turns into a everday man she can be Ava Maureen and if he sticks on to bein the Lord Jesus she can be his mammy. It ain't much reason to worry about her."

It was getting cooler and we had us a little breeze. On either side of the road they was land that had once been plowed but now it was growed up in weeds and bushes. It give you a lonely feeling to look at it, because you thought that all through here people use to live and now they was either dead or all gone off somewheres. I wondered where did they go. Maybe they was all like me and taken off for places like Manfred City and Birmingham and Detroit. People around Clearpoint— both nigger and white—was always going to Detroit because that's where they said the money was and everbody treated you like you was somebody. My pa had his own notions about Detroit. He said they wasn't a one of them—nigger or white—that went off up there that didn't finally come cowering back to Clearpoint with their tails stuck between their legs. They'd make the money sure enough, he said, and then they'd blow it as quick as they made it, and when they was broke they wasn't a friendly hand in all of Detroit to throw them a bite of bread—so here they come back to Clearpoint, where they had friends and relatives and where they was took care of when bad times come.

I had a Uncle Joe on my ma's side that done that very thing. Pa was usually right about his notions on living and what would happen to you if you done this or that. He had foresight in the way that ma had love and compassion.

Me and Bessie wasn't going very fast because I knowed she'd had a hard day. I straightened out her mane and patted her and told her she had a sight more endurance than most people I knowed, except for my close kinfolks.

Bessie could always tell what I was talking about. The Lord Jesus could have went on for eighty-eight hours telling me how fine his automobile the Dreama Glory was but it wouldn't of cut no ice with me. Bessie might not could make music or have winders to go up and down but she could get happy and could suffer and I could feel something that was alive to my legs when I was on her.

"Bessie," I said, "you ain't no dreama nothin. You're Bessie."

Then I spotted some green grass up the way and beyond it some woods.

"Looka yonder," I said. "You's goin to have grazin."

I set under a oak tree and leaned my back against the trunk while Bessie was nibbling at the grass. I pulled the ten-dollar bill out of my pocket and studied the picture on it of President Hamilton and of the U. S. Treasury on the back. It was the first ten-dollar bill I had ever owned. I had saved above ten dollars for Christmas presents and such, but it was in one-dollar bills.

I couldn't understand why Ava Maureen had just up and gave me this. Maybe it was like she said, that money was not no object. It seemed like it would of been more

like the Virgin Mary to give the ten-dollar bill than
Ava Maureen, but then I didn't know.

I got to daydreaming about what if I was a rich man
from New York City and in the mule business and I was
to come through Clearpoint and say to E. B. Lunsford,
"How much you take for them sixty acres you got?" and
him say, "They ain't enough money on this earth to buy
them sixty acres because they is good bottomland and it
was my own pa that cleared it," and then I would reach
in my pocket and hand him a stack of hundred-dollar
bills and say, "Will this here take care of it for you?" I
would go all around Clearpoint and neighboring towns
and buy up everthing. Then I would write to ma and
pa and Ed, Silas, Lamour Anne, and Naomi, who would
all be foreigners in New York City and all of them sad
there because they didn't know anybody and there was
so much traffic, and I'd say: "I got a whole town and the
surroundin countryside fer you. I got you milk cows and
chickens and all sech." They would be overjoyed. Pa
would think to hisself what a fine son he had and what a
good business head.

I went on with this kind of dreaming and went to
sleep. I didn't wake up till it was morning and getting
light.

Bessie was standing right in front of me and looking
down at me like she thought I'd had enough rest. Birds
of every nature was singing, and the air was so fresh and
good that I tried to pull as much of it into my lungs as I
could. It felt like it cleaned me out.

When I got up and stretched I felt some soreness in
my back but not enough to even thing about. All I felt
was good, and like this air and the pure blue sky and

71

them birds singing was all put here just for me and Bessie on this morning.

"We better be on the road, Bessie. The sun is gonna start gettin hot and we gotta find me a place to get some breakfast. I ain't use to one meal per day like I had yestiddy. If I'm still agrowin I got to have somethin to grow on."

The gravel road didn't seem so dry and dusty now while it was still fairly cool. But send one automobile through there and put a little sunshine to it and it would be so bad you couldn't hardly breathe.

I had made up my mind that I wasn't going to be in no special kind of hurry, now or at any time on my journey. They wasn't nothing to hurry to, Manfred City, but something to wait for you till you got there. They was things to hurry out of, if you knowed what was good for you, like the Lord Jesus Turner without his nail and the Virgin Mary when she turned into Ava Maureen and Oli-Oli and his tribe of converts if your hair didn't stand right. But them was things to get out of, which wasn't near so much effort as things to hurry up towards.

I was ruminating and spotted a house down the way to the right-hand side of the road that was painted white. I decided I'd stop and try to buy some breakfast out of my ten-dollar bill or else maybe do some handy work around the place to pay for it.

As I come up closer I could tell what a nice little farm place it was and how neat it was kept. The front yard all the way to the road was bright green grass. They was a small-sized barn in the back and some chicken houses. They wasn't any trash or old plows around them and the weeds was cut down.

A lady was setting on the front porch. I got off of Bessie and started leading her across the yard.

The woman put her hand up to her sunbonnet and hollered, "Take the hoss around to the back and tie it up thar," which I done, to a willow tree that was near the well.

I come on back around and the lady was shelling peas. She had a nice face and was right old, I'd say seventy-eighty, and what I could see of her hair sticking out from the sides of the bonnet was gray.

"Good mawnin," she said.

I told her howdy.

"Pull you up that cheer over there and set."

She had on a dark blue dress that was long, the way the old women around Clearpoint would wear them and like my ma's ma did before she died. She had on glasses without any rims, and she had a face that was awful thin but what you would call purty for somebody as old as she was.

I pulled up the chair and set down. It was one of them springing tin chairs like you see out in some people's yards.

"My name is Mary Dove Truman," she said and put out a little hand without hardly any flesh on it for me to shake.

We shaken and I said, "My name is Rover Youngblood, that's my mare Bessie in the back, and I'm glad to meet you."

"Looks like you're travelin," she said. She had a gentle voice but with a scrape to it because it was so old.

"Yes, ma'am, me and Bessie is off to Manfred City."

"I got a nephew that lives over there. My sister's boy.

73

Name of Duane Brown. He's in the funeral business. Why you out so early in the mawnin?"

"I slept on the roadside. I started out yestiddy."

"It ain't been much traffic lately, praise be the Lord."

"No, ma'am, it sure ain't."

She had a dishpan in her lap that she was shelling the peas in, and beside her was a sack where she dropped the empty shells. Her thumb would break the pod open and zip right through it, like she'd been shelling peas all of her life.

"Whur do you come from?" she wanted to know.

I told her and give her some of my past history.

"I ain't never been to Clearpoint but I've heared of it all of my life. A old nigger man by name of Amos that use to plow fer us come from Clearpoint or therabouts. He was always takin on and sayin folks didn't work you at Clearpoint like they did in this part of the country. I'd say to him, 'Make haste, Amos,' and he'd say, 'I's gwine make haste back to Clearpoint.' But he didn't. He's buried out yonder to the back of the house. What air you running off from?"

She give a quick look up over her glasses and then back down to her pea shelling.

"Varus things," I said. "One thing, me and my pa got into it. I reckin it's nature, because I ain't got nothin agin him."

She made a humming sound in her throat but no comment on what I said.

"Me and my husband never had us any younguns. It's a sorrow I've bore in my bosom but I reckin it's kept me from sorrow too. It's a sight how they do today: the girls smokin cigarettes and all of them goin to the picture

74

show. No respect fer marriage. I hope you have got respect fer marriage."

"Yes, ma'am," I told her. "I have thought about myself gettin married."

"Well, don't run into it and then out of it."

"I'm gonna try to make sure."

She stopped shelling peas and looked straight at me. "Did you know that light-colored hair weighs less than dark-colored hair?" She didn't stop to let me answer. "And did you know that the everday human bein that's got light-colored hair has got on the average of one hunnert and forty thousand hairs per head and that the brown-headed has got on the average of one hunnert and ten thousand hairs and the black-headed ain't got but one hunnert and three thousand?"

She'd asked the question like it was something I ought to be happy to find out about, so I tried to answer as strong as I could and make it sound like I was awful happy to find out what she told me.

"I never would of thought that, ma'am. They's a big differnce between the black-headed and the light, ain't they? I wonder if you could tell the differnce if you was black-headed and changed to light-headed?"

"Like as not," she said and went back to shelling peas.

I said, "They's a lots of things on this earth I ain't never heared of. I learnt that goin to school. I went through the sixth grade."

"You ought to awent on."

"Had to work," I told her.

"Well, it's work and wars and if it ain't that it's sickness. My old husband lays in yonder now in the bed-

75

room, won't get up, and has got him the mind of a two-year-old baby. One day his right mind jest up and left him, like it was a tenant farmer that had moved in and then one night unbeknownst to all, moved away and never heared hide nor hair of since.

"His name is Joe Two Truman. Called Joe Two because he had a brother got kilt before he was born, by bein throwed by a horse, and *his* name was Joe. So then come along my husband and his old ma wanted to name him Joe Two, she was still so grieved over Joe One. I got rheumatism in my hands."

She stretched out her arms and moved her fingers the best she could.

"He just lays there and mumbles and says ugly words and acts like he don't know me. We been livin together all of our lives. And he begs for peppermint candy. I give him the peppermint candy ever oncet in a while but they ain't no collard greens. He likes them too. What was yore name?"

"Rover Youngblood."

"It don't pay to get old, Rover. Don't never get old." She wasn't looking up.

"No, ma'am." But didn't see how I could keep from it unless they was something terrible happened to me.

"Did yore teacher in the school ever learn you any poems or make you recite them?"

"Two–three," I said. "I warn't never much good at it. I was always timid to get up in front of others."

"Say me somethin you learnt."

Right then I couldn't remember nothing. Then the first three lines of Sidney Lanier's "Corn" come to me and I said:

Today the woods are tremblin through and through
With shimmerin forms that flash before my view,
Then melt in green, as day-stars melt in blue.

I didn't tell Miss Mary Dove Truman that I didn't
have no more notion than a billy goat what all them
words was trying to get at.

"Ain't that beautiful," she said. She waved a fly away
from her and went on. "I'm a poet myself. I been setting
down verses since I was a youngun and have got my life
and that of my kinfolks in sech a way recorded. I been
published in varus newspapers, includin the Manfred
City *Democrat.*" She taken one hand from the peas and
pointed at me. "They ain't nothin to relieve you so
much as verses, whether you be in sorrow, sickness, or
taxes. And it helps the work go fast. I got verses to go
with everthing I work at. When I'm washin up the
dishes I say:

> Wash a cup and dry a cup
> And put them all away.
> Now you got your dishes done
> Fer another day.

I wrote that myself, and if you ever got any dishes to
wash, say them lines and it won't be no time till you're
through with the dishes and you hadn't even thought
about it.

"I got this here that I say when I work in the garden:

> When I plant my beans and corn

77

> I must chop out ever thorn.
> When I plant my lettuce green
> Not a rabbit shall be seen.
> Choppy-chop and dig-dig-dig.
> All I plant will grow up big.

It keeps the rabbits off too."

I didn't want to interrupt Miss Mary Dove's verses but I knowed that if she had one for everthing she done during the day, we might be setting there a day's time and I wouldn't have no breakfast till tomorrow.

"Do you reckin I could pay you or do some handy work around the house here to get me some breakfast?" I said right quick while she was getting her breath.

"You pore innocent youngun," she said, "me asettin here and rollin off verses and you ain't eat. You set right here and go on with shellin the peas and I'll go to the kitchen and cook you up somethin hearty."

She groaned getting up and then handed the pan and such to me.

"I got the bounty of the earth from my barn, chicken house, and garden. I share with others even if I ain't a Commonist.

> Put some stove wood on the fire.
> But don't ever be a liar.
> Cook the vittles till they're done.
> Standin here is really fun.

That's what I say when I cook."

She went in the house and didn't slam the screen but

let it to easy. On the screen she had some balls of cotton to scare off the flys.

I must of shelled for ten minutes before she come back to the door and said, "I got it settin on the table fer you."

She led me through the living room to the kitchen, which was neat and clean as you ever saw, with a wood stove, a pantry, a table and four chairs painted white, a churn, some cabinets, red peppers hanging on a string from the wall, a gourd dipper on a nail, a calendar with a picture of a red-headed gal smiling so's you could see her teeth big and advertising Dundee (Oh, it's so good!) Snuff.

I set down to a feast and she said, "If it ain't good enough fer you and yore belly still is empty, let me know and I'll cook up some more." Then she laughed and watched to see how I'd like it.

I liked it fine. She had store-bought loaf bread and sorghum, thick bacon, a plate of fresh ripe tomatoes, scrambled eggs, coffee, and all the grits you could eat. It nearly made me ache it was so good.

"What you do to get groceries and sech that you don't raise on the place here?" I asked.

"Why, they is this old gentleman by the name of Mr. Ulris Sparkman that lives about a mile down in back off of this main road. He is a old bachelor gentleman and oncet a week on Satady he drives his pickup to Adlet, Alabama, and gets his staples and mine fer me. That's when I buy Mr. Joe Two's peppermints. We draw a pension on the First Great War."

I told her I had a cousin by the name of Rust Young-

79

blood that drawed a pension on the Second Great War because he got his left foot blowed off.

"Mr. Joe Two got sharpnel pierced all through his chest and it's still there. That might be what's rurnt his mind. In the First Great War they was fifty-three thousand and four hunnert and seven killed in battle. That's a sight, ain't it? I can praise the Lord that Mr. Joe Two Truman warn't kilt even if he was filled up with sharpnel."

I was thinking to myself that Miss Mary Dove had more facts and numbers than anybody I'd ever heared about.

"How can you remember all sech as that?" I asked her. "All them numbers about hairs on the head and folks kilt in the wars."

She tapped the side of her head with one of her crooked fingers. "I got a magnetic mind. Ain't nothin goes in but what stays. They's things in there that ain't no use to me and I'd as soon shet off but they's other things I like to study over and is a comfort to me when I'm here and ain't got nobody to talk to. Don't you like to study back on life when you're by yourself?"

I told her I did but that I didn't have much to study over when it come to numbers and a lot of memorizing. "I study over things like huntin squirrels and treein possums, like I use to do with my brothers and sometimes with my pa. I ain't learnt enough to study back much."

"Hit'll come to you," she said and got up and said, "Scuse me," and went out of the room and come back in with what she told me was a radio, about three-quarter as long as your outstretched hand and a inch and a half thick, without no wires to connect it up. She said it run on batteries. She said you could take it with you anywhere you wanted to, in your pocket or what, and it would play right along for you as long as the batteries was all right.

When she turned it on it made a popping and growling sound till she got a man who was talking about the rain and how much percent of a area it was going to cover that night.

"Thought I might get the war news," she said. "They always close up with the weather. We need the rain. That there's Manfred City you jest heared. Comes in clear, don't it? I got me two radios like this. One was bought by Mr. Joe Two and one was give to me by my nephew in the funeral business over at Manfred City. He's a right nice boy even if he does gang up with the IIIUN."

She clicked off the radio and set it on the table.

I said, "What's the IIIUN?"

"By the name of Duane Brown," she said.

"Ma'am?"

"Duane Brown is the name of my nephew in the funeral business."

"Yes, ma'am. What is the IIIUN?" I was spreading some sorghum on a piece of loaf bread.

"Them letters fer these here words: *I'm* what *I* think *I* am, *You're Not*. It's somethin close to the Klu Klux Klan. Ride around with sacks and sheets and sech over their heads."

I knowed what the Klu Klux Klan was because I'd seen them coming through Clearpoint in their sheets with nose, mouth, and eyes cut out, and riding both cars

81

and horses. Then the niggers had also told me stories.

"They is a sight," Miss Mary Dove said. "The iiiun. Wouldn't give you a nickel fer the bunch of them. They come through here on this road and tack up their circlers on the trees as to when they are plannin a meetin. I have went up and down the road in either direction and taken down ever circler I seen, because it ruins the look of the trees, fer one thing, and I ain't got total sympathy fer their ways is another."

Miss Mary Dove poured me some more coffee and I asked her, "What all do they do?"

"Anything that was to come into their mind."

She told me the next in a whisper, leaning towards me: "I can speak from havin lived and sawed and heared, as to the iiiun. They is like a bunch of chilrun that likes to dress up and hide their faces and get into all kinds of devilment as long as they've got a whole crowd of other chilrun to rip and snort and back them up. They ain't a one of them that would take the flour sack off of his head and stand by hisself."

Miss Mary Dove pulled off her glasses and cleaned them on the hem of her dress.

"When you have got chilrun, you have got to treat them like chilrun. The iiiun folks is chilrun. Don't care how old they air in years. Did you ever have a club or gang?"

I told her that me and Ed and Silas had a club we called the Snake Chasers. What you had to do was catch a snake alive and show it to me, who was the president, to get into the club. It was better if it was a poison snake, but it didn't have to be. Ed never could of got in because he wouldn't handle nothing but the green garden snake.

You had to cut off the snake's head, put it in a fruit jar, and sleep with it next to you at night for a week. Ma throwed Silas's out when she found it one morning sweeping.

"I would call the roll," I told Miss Mary Dove. "Silas was secatery and would write down the name of anybody that was missin. Then we'd say our slogan which was this: I ain't afraid of no snake on earth, whuther it's ten inches long or ten foot. I am gonna handle snakes fer the rest of my life and to scare as many folks as I can. Kinfolks is left out. Amen."

Miss Mary Dove wanted to know why kinfolks was left out.

"We'd get a whuppin," I told her. Ma did not care nothing for snakes and my sisters would scream and take on if they ever seen one. Pa never let on much about them. He said some was good and some was bad. The black ones was useful.

I said, "After the roll call and the slogan we'd have to run off through the woods, down by the branch whur it looked snaky, barefooted and with our overalls rolled up, circle three times, and run back to the pine tree whur our club was at. At night we'd lay in bed and make up snake stories. Sometimes Silas would be so afraid he'd have to get in bed with me."

"I ain't never cared fer snakes," Miss Mary Dove said. "Other day when I was hoein I kilt a copperhead. It's hangin on the clothesline now. What come of yore club?"

"It got to be winter and didn't seem much use in goin on with it."

She asked me, "Would you mind if I was to take a dip of snuff?"

I told her that no ma'am I wouldn't.

She went off to the living room and come back with her can of snuff, a sweetgum brush, and a jar to spit in with a brown paper sack around it.

"Did you know," she started off and I knowed she was going to give me some kind of fact or figure that I didn't know, "that what they use fer money in Korear is called *hwan* and that in 1938 they had five thousand and three hunnert Christians?"

I told her that was sure a lot of Christians.

"I got it on the war news when we was fightin at Korear. They's a lots you can pick up on the radio. Airplane crashes, floods, tornadies."

"My fambly had a radio oncet," I said, "but lightnin run in on it so's it wouldn't play no more."

"It cain't run in on this kind. You go on out to the porch whur it's cool. I'll see about Mr. Joe Two. See if he wants some peppermint."

I went outside and set down and looked at Miss Mary Dove's two beds of zinnias and marigolds. At both ends of the porch she had morning glories climbing on strings. Around the edges of the porch in Swift lard buckets she had ferns and petunias blooming. You could tell just by how she taken a interest in everthing what kind of a good old lady she was.

"Mr. Joe Two said he was gonna spend the rest of his life on this earth in a picture show," Miss Mary Dove told me when she set down. "He ain't been to but one picture show in his entire life, with Shirley Temple and Will Rogers in it. That's the shape his mind is in. He wants to do everything that's bad."

84

"Most folks goes the other way," I said.

She'd brought some crocheting with her and was jabbing away with the needles. I'd finished up the peas myself.

"How's that?" she asked me.

"Most folks do everthing that's bad before they get old and sick, and then they start to repent and prepare fer the next life. He's doin it bass-ackerds." It come out of my mouth before I knowed it and I was ashamed of myself.

"Scuse me."

"I've heared worse." She didn't even look up from her crocheting. "When I was at a meetin of the ɪɪɪᴜɴ, I heared talk not fit fer mules to hear."

I was about to ask her what she was doing at a place like that but I didn't have to. She proceeded on to tell me.

"I knowed they was gonna have a meetin down in the woods t'other side of the road, so I taken into my head that I'd sneak up and watch and see what all went on. About nine o'clock at night cars and trucks started parkin over yonder and hosses hitched up to the trees. About nine-thirty I walked down the road a piece and cut into the woods, then come back thisaway. They was at a clearin and had a big fire goin. All of them with their headpieces and robes and sech. Some with sheets and some with bathrobes. Must of been forty-five to fifty settin around in a hafa circle and four standin up to face the rest beyond the firs.

"The one that was in charge had a hatchet in his hand, was runnin back and forth and hollerin so's I could of heared him on this porch: *'To all of them that ain't: I'm what I think I am, You're Not.'* 'Whoopee,' all that was

85

settin down said. *'I am a law unto myself.'* 'Whoopee.' And they went on with sech childishness as that fer a while. Then one of the men standin up give some kind of a report, told how many niggers had been scared in the last week, told how much money was on hand, and ast everbody there to put a dollar in a shoe box before they left. It seemed like they was plannin on havin a social, because all the wives was invited."

I was enjoying all this talk about the IIIUN and not thinking about much of anything when my eyes come to light on a red automobile without no top lickety-splitting it down the road from my left. I jumped up and got in the house, behind the screen. I knowed it would be the Lord Jesus out looking for me and his nail.

"Rover, what is it?" Miss Mary Dove said.

"It ain't nothin. Jest set whur you are. I don't want who's in that automobile to see me."

It went past and sure enough it was the Lord Jesus, and the Virgin was setting next to him. He must of been going seventy-eighty miles an hour because a cloud of dust so thick you could cut it come sailing right for the house.

I went back on the porch and set down with Miss Mary Dove to breathe the dust.

"I met that man yestiddy and don't care to see him no more," I told her.

"He was in a hurry fer somethin."

"Yes, ma'am. Go on and tell me about the IIIUN."

"Well, varus ones of them told about their relations with nigger women and what I taken to be po white trash women. I ain't never listened to sech language in my life and hold it a sin on my soul that I listened as long as I did. After while a man brought up a chicken that was makin a mighty racket, to the man with the hatchet. Another man standin there beside him helped him hold the chicken down while he chopped off its head. The man with the hatchet slung it around in the air by its legs so's that blood went flyin in ever direction, some landin on them that was settin. Then he held the chicken up to him and let blood run all down the front of his sheet. You never seen sech a mess. He throwed the chicken in the fire and got down on his knees and bowed his head to it.

"He hollered, *'By this blood and what it repasents of the blood we have spilt and the blood we will spill I swear my soul to the* IIUN *and all of its laws and what it repasents in the name of God Amighty. Repeat.'* All the others repeated it.

"That there was all I could stand. Chicken blood and blasphemin to God. I snuck back through the woods and come on home to lock my door. Hit were a sight and one I don't look forward to nomore."

Some kind of squealing racket come from inside the house and Miss Mary Dove up and went to see about it. I taken it to be Mr. Joe Two, which it was.

Miss Mary Dove said from inside, "He heared us talkin and wants to see who the company is. Come on in, Rover, so's he can look at you."

I did. I went into the bedroom where he was laying on a bed in his nightshirt and was propped up on pillows. She had him clean and neat and he didn't look like his mind was gone. He had white hair and a white handlebar moustache. They was a picture of him and her when they was young hanging on the wall over his head.

"What's yore name, boy?" he asked me.

I told him it was Rover Youngblood.

"Goddamit, I ast what was yore name."

"Rover Youngblood," I said.

Miss Mary Dove whispered to me, "Pay no mind to his cussin. He never said a cuss word in his life till he got like this."

"What you sayin to that boy, woman whore?" Mr. Joe Two said.

"I was tellin him how good peppermint candy is."

"Yer wantin to lay with him, that's what."

Miss Mary Dove let out a groan and said she was going to the front porch. She said for me to stay and keep him company for a little bit.

I set down in a chair where he could see me.

He said, "When I get outa this bed I'm goin to the picture show and spend my entire life thar. Whatta you think of that?"

I couldn't think of nothing to answer so I asked him what shows he wanted to see.

He told me he wanted to see Shirley Temple and Will Rogers and he went on: "I'm gonna set thar with a bottle of homebrew and stay drunk ever minute, goddamit, and when I get tired of that I'm gonna lay in the floor with a whore woman. Whatta you think of that?"

I told him he'd have to stop ever now and again to eat and take a bath.

"I'll rurn my belly and stay nasty as a hog. Whatta you think of that?"

Just then Miss Mary Dove hollered from the front porch that I'd stayed long enough and for me to come on. I was glad because I was having a hard time thinking of answers to give to Mr. Joe Two.

I said, "It was good to meet you, Mr. Joe Two."

"Goddamit, whur you goin?"

He was still saying goddamit when I got out to the porch.

"The Umpire State Building," Miss Mary Dove said without looking up and going right on with her crocheting, "is the tallest building in America, with one hunnert and two stories and a height of one thousand and two hunnert and fifty foot. The Arctic Ocean is the fourth biggest of the oceans and the seas, and the Angel Waterfall is the tallest on earth."

Then she didn't say nothin, and I finally said, "Miss Mary Dove, I'm gonna take Bessie and be on down the road. I'd enjoy settin here and talkin to you all day but it wouldn't hep me on my journey. You've been awful nice to me. That was close to the best breakfast I ever eat."

She stood up and pressed out her dress and set her crocheting down on the chair.

"You take the hoss out to the barn," she said, "and give her some hay. I'll be fixing you up a lunch to take."

Miss Mary Dove walked me and Bessie to the road. She had my lunch in a lard bucket, and she'd brought a piece of thin rope for me to hang over Bessie, with the lunch on one side and my clothes that was in the chicken feed sack on the other.

"I hope to see you in the future," Miss Mary Dove said.

"I hope to see you in the future too, Miss Mary Dove. And I hope Mr. Joe Two gets better."

I thanked her again and struck off.

When I looked back she waved at me and I waved.

Bless her heart, I said to myself, her standing there

in her bonnet and her old-folks dress and her looking about the size you could put her in your hand and hold her.

Then she hollered, "Rover!"

I stopped Bessie and turned.

"Come back here a minute."

I did and she said, "I fergot to tell you my travelin verse."

It went like this:

> When you hit the dusty road
> Never take a heavy load.
> Leave your worries at the door.
> Look ahead to what's in store.
> If it's relatives you see
> Always let their fighting be.
> If you go to buy a hat
> Never buy no more than that.
> Under clothes your money pin.
> There is folks don't mind to sin.
> Laugh and talk and sing away.
> When it's night, then stop to pray.

She added to that: "Did you know that the Duke of Windsor married Wallis Warfield Simpson on June 3, 1937?"

I told her I didn't but that I knowed they was a Duchess of Windsor. Ma use to mention her from time to time.

We said good-bye again, and then me and Bessie taken off for sure.

90

Chapter 10

I HAD IT in my head that I'd be ready to head into field, pasture, or woods if I was to catch a sight of the Lord Jesus Turner. He could outrun me on the road but the Dreama Glory wouldn't be much help to him after he got off of it.

The sun was a great big white-hot ball striking down at me and Bessie. It looked like the growth along the sides of the road had already give up for the day, and was drooping and dusty-looking. Sweat was rolling down my back and Bessie was lathering.

"Bessie," I said, "I'd give my nail that pierced the palm of Jesus Christ fer a Coca-Cola. I'd give half of this lunch that Miss Mary Dove fixed up if it was to come a good shower and drench us both down to the skin. I'd give my Sunday shoes if it was to come a snowstorm."

Speaking of Coca-Colas, I thought to myself that Silas

91

and Ed both liked orange, peach, or strawberry the best and Naomi and Lamour Anne both liked grape and chocolate. I was the one that stuck up for the Coca-Cola for several reasons: (1) I liked the taste of it and I'd heared they wasn't nobody but them that made it that knowed what was put into it; (2) if you drunk it fast it would make a burning to your tongue that I liked; (3) sometimes if I felt run-down or had a headache or felt groggy in general I'd take a Coca-Cola and sometimes a aspirin but sometimes not and then would feel better and more like doing my chores; (4) it give you something to do and wouldn't leave a bad taste in your mouth like a peach or strawberry drink might; (5) if you got some bad homebrew a Coca-Cola was good to follow it up with.

Ma would take a Coca-Cola ever now and again. She said they helped to settle her stomach and made her sleep good at night. Pa was just the opposite. He said they kept him awake. But he didn't care much for any kind of a drink but buttermilk and coffee without sugar in it.

We was going down a little hill and I noticed at the top of the next one a filling station or what appeared to be.

I said, "Bessie, if you can make the climb we'll take us a rest and cool off."

When we got there I seen they was having a sale on gas. SKY ROCKET LOW PRICES, a sign said that was strung out on a wire from the front of the station to a pole out near the road. They was two pumps in front of the two-story building that was covered with all description of signs: GOOD (and a foot with wings on it) YEAR, AC FARM TRACTOR HEAVY DUTY SPARK PLUGS, BAYER ASPIRIN, HAIR CARE WITH EXTRA DUTY ACTION, COCA-COLA, NEHI, ROYAL CROWN, and on like that. They wasn't anybody setting outside but they was two pickups and a old model Ford with the color green nearly faded off of it. To the back where you could see a outhouse, some sheds that looked propped up and about to fall, a bunch of automobile parts and general trash, they was a old truck with the back of it slumped to the side.

After I'd fastened Bessie to what was left of a fence post, I started to the screen door of the filling station and could hear voices talking inside. The screens was covered with about two thousand flies and they had on them signs advertising Martha Washington Bread.

I walked in to find four men setting, three on cane-bottom chairs and one on a wood box.

"Howdy," the one setting on the wood box said. He stood up. "Is it anything I can do fer you?"

He come down straight, not fat, to his belly and then it shot out all of a sudden like it was a bad growth. His nose had a crook to it and his face was about the color of new butter. I taken him to be the owner of the station.

"I been ridin my hoss," I said, "and I wanted to rest and have me a Coca-Cola."

He opened up the cold-drink box and I could see the vegetables and other things stored on the ice to keep fresh.

He handed me my Coca-Cola and then a wood box like his from behind the counter. The inside of the sta-

93

tion was a grocery store but fairly low on what it had to sell. Mainly snuff and cigarettes and chewing tobacco along with some canned goods.

"Set down," the man said to me, "and rest from the heat."

They went on to talking about what they must of been talking about when I come in, having to do with a old man by the name of Mr. Billy Bull Taylor who had set fire to a woman's house and got throwed in county jail by the sheriff. They was all laughing about it. It seemed like Mr. Billy Bull wasn't married to this old woman but stayed with her and he wouldn't work none but run off and got drunk all the time. He'd come in not long ago, way past midnight, drunk and making a racket and climbed into bed stripped off neckid with the old woman. She wanted to know if maybe he didn't want a nice cup of hot coffee so's maybe he wouldn't feel so bad in the morning. Old Mr. Billy Bull laid there with the walls swimming before him and thought how fine it was the old woman hadn't bawled him out and had taken a interest in how he might feel tomorrow. She'd come back in the room with a cup of coffee so hot it was steaming and said in a voice sweet as Christmas pie, "Here's yore coffee, sugar," and then proceeded to pour it on his privates. Old Mr. Billy Bull run out of the house to the woods and laid across a branch with his privates in it.

When he got to feeling better he set fire to the old woman's house but she got it put out. That's how come he was arrested by the sheriff and throwed in county jail.

All four of the men was slapping their knees.

"Fus time he's been sober in ten year," one man said

that had a old felt hat on his head that was turned down
all the way around. His mouth was drawed down so he
looked in pain even though he was laughing.

"If him and Sheriff Barton ain't settin there havin
homebrew together," the owner of the place said, "Ottie
Sam Barton likes his nip as good as anybody."

"And gets it more too, by raidin the stills." This one
that spoke looked a good deal younger than the others
and had on overalls without a shirt. He'd cut hisself on
the neck at what I figured to of been shaving. His chin
come way out, and the rest of his face and head sloped
back gradual.

"He's offered to sell it to me," the owner said.

The man in the felt hat spit tobacco juice in a can
and said, "Hell's fire, anybody that taken a notion, from
one year up to eighty, could go by noon daylight and
buy as much as he wanted to if he'd pay cash on the
barrel."

"That's so," the young one said.

The fourth man hadn't spoke a word. His hair was
parted in the middle and it looked like it hadn't been
cut for a long time. They wasn't much expression to his
face and his eyes was dark but didn't have much shine to
them.

He said to me, "You totin lots of money fer a young
boy."

He was referring to me having give my ten-dollar bill
to the owner when I got my Coca-Cola.

I told him it was a right smart more money than I was
use to. I said that I never had owned a ten-dollar bill
before and hated to see it go.

He looked at me blank but with what come close to

95

being a look saying "I don't believe you" or "If I do believe you, I ain't got much use fer you."

"Did you work fer it?" he said.

"It was give to me."

The young one wanted to know where I was heading.

When I told him Manfred City, he said, "I worked there at a body shop after the war at Korea. Hit's a lots to do thar and a lots of purty gals. I know, cause it's whar I got the clap."

The others grinned, including the one that looked in pain.

"Watch out fer house number 1002 on Sun Flower Street with a party by name of Betty Nell Fields. If you don't want to get a dose."

I told him I didn't want no clap, thinking to myself if that was what a dose was.

When I told them I was from Clearpoint the man with the hat on said he'd made a cotton crop around there about twenty year ago but he didn't do no good with it and seemed like everything went wrong. His cow died and his old sow eat up all of her pigs.

The man with long hair said, "What air you goin to do at Manfurd City?"

"Try to get some kind of a job. I'm purty good with hosses."

"Ain't no call fer hosses at Manfurd City," he said and taken a match he'd been playing with and chewed a piece off of it.

I had a feeling he was just as glad there weren't no calling for hosses.

The owner said that he was gonna have to go to Manfred City in a week or two to see about trading his truck on a car of some kind. He said the truck was about to draw its last breath.

I spoke to the owner of the place and said, "Have you saw anybody come along here today in a red convertible automobile, like as not wearing black clothes and with a woman wearing black clothes?"

"Shore," he said. "The Lord Jesus Turner and the Virgin Mary. I give him some gas fer puttin a blessing on my sick calf out yonder in back. He had him a load of homebrew his niggers made to take to Manfurd City. He warn't in no kind of mood. Said the blessin over the calf so quick I don't know if it'll take or not. Wallace"— and he pointed to the young man—"was here when he come through."

"I was here," Wallace said. "The Virgunt didn't look in no kind of mood neither. I said to her, 'Virgunt, how is the healin and prayin and works of the Lord?' and she told me to hesh up before she damned me to Pergertory. I wusht I had a car like they got."

"Hit'll do ninety mile a hour and above," the man with the hat said. "Oncet the Lord Jesus give me a ride in it. We throwed up dust so's you couldn't see behind you. Hit's air-cooled too."

The man that didn't like me said, "I'd as soon to have my old pickup out there. It ain't so complicated and ain't so many things to go wrong with hit. If one of them revolvin winders gets broke, Lord Jesus has got to drive all the way to Manfurd City and order off fer a part. If they comes rain or hail while he's waitin, it goes right in at the winder and ain't nothin you can do about it. If that there top gets stuck in midway, ain't nothin you can do but have it there like a sail to cut down on yore speed till you find a athority to get it down fer you. Same thing with that there radio. If you get it to playin and it sticks on you, you got to listen to it till the battery runs down. I ain't got no sech problems as that with my pickup." He give his head a kind of jerk, like he was proud to be so well off.

The young man named Wallace said, "Lord Jesus wanted to know if it was anybody had come by here ridin on a hoss."

I started not to let on about Bessie being tied outside, but then I thought they'd like as not see her or else hear her make a racket and if I didn't speak up they might suspect something about me.

"Why, I got a hoss that I'm ridin on," I said, trying to act surprised and looking around from one face to the other.

"You know the Lord Jesus?" the owner asked me.

"I don't know him to speak of but I am a admirer of his automobile. First one I ever seen like that."

"Hit's the latest model," he said.

Then they all got off to talking about the government and what a mess it was in. One thought a judge on the Supreme Court was a Communist. Somebody agreed with him. Somebody else said that the next President was sure to be a nigger and Catholic combined with probably some Jew blood. The man with the hat said that plain Americans like him would like as not be throwed out of the country and be moved to Africa so that the Africans could come over here. Wallace didn't think it would come to that but thought it was bad. The owner told him he didn't know because he was young and hadn't lived and saw as much as the rest of them had. The man with long hair started to tell what it was like in the Great Depression.

I wasn't paying much mind to what they was saying, just letting my mind wander and looking around the store. I heard a door from upstairs open and shut, then heard somebody coming down the steps because the steps was creaking, and then standing at the door to where the steps went up at the back of the room was this purty gal standing there that looked to be about twelve-fourteen and with bosoms that was a knockout. I taken her to be the daughter of the owner. She stood there and looked at me and grinned, and I finally looked down at the floor and then looked back at her.

She put up her finger and crooked it and moved it for me to come on. Then she winked at me and grinned some more. The men was still going on about the Great Depression, telling Wallace what all he'd missed. I didn't know what to do about the gal. She kept crooking her finger and winking.

Either the men seen me looking at the gal or else they caught all of the motion she was making out of the corner of their eyes, whichever, they all turned around to look at her. She done a kind of dip and said in a voice that wavered up and down, "Hi!"

We all said howdy.

"What're you up to, Ursula?" the owner wanted to know.

"Nothin. What's that boy's name?"

"He ain't spoke his name. He's headed fer Manfurd City."

"Oh," she said. "I have spent a major part of my life there."

99

"You better be glad you're here so's you can be took care of."

I thought maybe he was separated from his wife and taking care of the daughter.

"I don't know. I seen a good bit of the world there." When she talked she drawed it and kind of whined, not like she was unhappy but like she was fidgeting.

"I think he's just fabulous," she said, speaking of me. "Just darlin! Cain't he come upstairs and hear some of my records?"

"He don't want to hear none of yore records." Then to me, "Do you?"

I sort of shrugged my shoulders.

She frowned and whimpered a little while and she said, "I'm gettin awful lonesome out here in the middle of nowhur on earth and about to swelter in the heat and don't have no entertainment at all, not to speak of the flies that keep comin in the hole in that screen that you said you would fix which you did not. I been nearly takin a notion to go off to Manfred City for some night life. If there is anything on this earth that I do hate to do it is to go to bed before the chickens and then have to listen to somebody snore. It makes me want to stand up and scream."

As she had talked on she'd worked herself to a pitch.

"Go on up thar and hear two or three of her records," the owner said to me.

None of the other men spoke a word.

I got up with all of them looking at me and went over to where Ursula was standing, then followed her up the stairs.

When we was at the top and into the room, she shut

the door and throwed her arms around me and said, "Oh, God!" Then I put my arms around her and we kissed.

Ursula pulled off and set down in a pink chair with ruffles on it. "Well, this is my room. How do you like it?"

I said, "Jest fine," and started to look around.

The room was all dolled up, with a dresser that had a pink cloth around it to the floor and above it a mirror and on it various kinds and colors of jars, bottles, boxes, and so on. The bed had a pink silky-looking spread with lots of different colored round and square pillows scattered about. On a table they was a wind-up phonograph something like my Cousin Felicity had at Clearpoint and beside it a stack of records. Besides all this she had a cedar chest with three teddy bears that was backed off by pictures of what I taken to be movie stars on the wall. They didn't look like everday people.

"That," she said and pointed to a door that was shut, "is *his* room. He just about bores me to death. But don't you like *my* room?"

I told her again that I did.

"I think it's darlin. I picked everthing out that's in here. Includin the cedar chest which is to keep my winter clothes nice and fresh. Do you like Elvis records? Set down on the bed."

I did and said, "What kind of records is that?"

"*Elv*is," she said. "Elvis Presley. He's a singer. He's *fab*ulous. I adore him."

I had not ever heared of who she was talking about but I told her I would be glad to listen.

She wound up the machine and put on a record. I

studied her while she was doing this. Her hair was so light-colored it looked nearly white, and I wondered if it was by nature. She had on a orange skirt and a white blouse that come down low so you could see the beginning of her bosoms. Her face was painted but not too much, and she sure did look nice. I had a tingling feeling come to me.

The record she put on had to do with a hound dog, which the singer said over and over.

"Do you like it?"

I told her that I liked it all right.

"I just love it," she said. "I think it's *fabu*lous. Sometimes I play it five or six times in a row."

I was hoping she wouldn't do that now.

"He is *so* sexy. He nearly kills me." Ursula had a way of talking that made her sound like she was excited all of the time.

"Who?" I asked her.

"*El*vis. That *sing*in. Who do you think?" Ursula also had a way of putting special stress to words and parts of words.

"You shore look fine, the way you're fixed up and everthing," I said and like as not turned red.

"You think so?" She put on a big smile. "You're darlin."

She went over to the cedar chest and lifted the top enough to pull out a bottle.

"This here," she said, "ain't none of that cheap homebrew that will rot your stomach out. This is store whisky that I bought in Manfred City and paid a big price for. Take a swaller."

I did and it was smooth and good. Then she hoisted

102

the bottle up and taken a long pull. I thought to myself that she was mighty young for a girl to be such a hand with whisky.

She wiped off her mouth with her hand and said, "Ain't that delicious?"

The record was finished but was still going around. She put on another one sung by a boy that sounded like he was crying or about to cry, and it had to do with him going to a dance and falling in love with this here gal he seen for the first time. She got cold so he gave her his sweater. Then he taken her home and left her there but later on remembered that she still had his sweater. Then he went back and was met at the door by the gal's pa that told him his daughter had died a year ago that day. Something strange drawed him to the graveyard to the gal's grave, and there he seen his sweater on it. The song didn't go on to say if he taken it or not.

Ursula said, "I just love that record. It makes me shiver all over."

"Do you reckin he was dancin with a corpse?" I asked.

"You ain't suppose to study it too close. It takes away the joy of it. Take another nippy-nip."

She handed me the bottle and I taken a bigger drink this time.

"That shore beats homebrew," I said. "When I get to Manfred City and find a job I'm gonna buy me some whisky like that."

I was already beginning to feel good and I wished I could stay there in that room with Ursula for the rest of my life.

Ursula said, "I bet you don't know what I want to do?"

103

She lit a cigarette and I couldn't help but think it would stunt her growth, her being a girl. But she was already growed up in body, so it didn't matter if she was stunted or not. If her bosoms got too much bigger she'd look deformed.

"Don't you care fer a cigarette?" she said.

I told her I didn't smoke but that I use to smoke rabbit tobacco.

"This here is a new filter kind and you can taste the tobacco like it was a real cigarette. Well, what I want to do"—and she stretched out her body in the chair and pulled her arms back so's I could see she'd shaved under her arms—"is to become either a movie star or sing on records. I think I'd ruther be a movie star. See all them pictures on the wall thar? Tab Hunter and Debbie Reynolds and Tony Curtis and Elvis and Frankie Avalon and Elizabeth Taylor." She let out a long heave of breath that could have been suffering but I knowed she meant it to be happiness. "She's my *i*deal. And *I* don't hold nothin against her about her private life and boy friends and marriages."

"How come you want to be a movie star?" I asked Ursula.

"Oh, they's too many reasons fer me to put it all in words. Might take a week to explain. Tha glamour of it, fer one thing. You know, to lay up on a big feather bed that was covered in satin and have a nigger woman or maybe even a white woman to stand there and fan you and throw chocolate candy in your mouth if you as much as wiggled your big toe. I think it would be fabulous. I may go out there."

I asked, "Whur?"

"To Hollywood, silly, and get discovered. I think I got what it takes and I *shore* know what to do with it.

"I'd like this here great big house with thirty or forty rooms to it and all the walls painted red and red rugs on the floor. And here's somethin I've thought up of my own that I ain't ever heard of a movie star doin when they was havin everthin to match: to have red water! How would you like that? Wouldn't that be *fab*ulous?"

I didn't say so but I didn't think I'd like it. It would make me think they was rust in the water.

"God, I love red. Don't you? And I would have a red car like Lord Jesus Turner has got but mine would be bigger and I'd have a man to drive me around and him dressed in red. Ever picture I was to appear in would have to have lots of red backdrops."

I said, "You might get tired of so much red. It might start to get on yore nerves. How come you got pink in here and not red?"

"Because I'm savin red for when I get to Hollywood or start singin on records. I got a good voice and won second prize in a amateur contest sponsored by the Civitan Club in Manfred City. Let me sing you the song I sung."

She turned off the record player and stood with her back to the mirror. While she was singing she done things with her hands and made several kinds of expressions with her face. It went like this:

> My love is like a whirlpool of desire,
> Something says my love will never tire.
> The birds all say,

105

The flowers say
You're everthing I ever will require.

Don't ever leave me,
Never deceive me,
Always retrieve me,
Love.

My love is like a oak tree growing high,
My love is always reaching to the sky.
The chulrun say,
The old folks say
My love is like two wings that forward fly.

Don't ever hate me,
Never debate me,
Always instate me,
Love.

Ursula finished off with the bowing of her head and
her arms stretched out to the sides.

"How do you like it?"

I told her I liked it fine and she ought to go far with
her voice.

"It was some silly little gal that done imitations of
farm animals that got the first prize in the contest. Her
daddy was mayor of Manfred City so they had to let her
win. Mr. Earl Cranton was one of the judges and told me
I was by a long shot the best. How far can you get in
Hollywood by imitatin a pig?"

I told her that I thought singing would go better with
picture shows or records either one than farm animal
imitations. They was only a certain amount of farm

animals you could imitate and then you was through
with that particular territory. Folks would like as not
get tired of it if you was to go on doing the same thing
over and over. On the other hand, they was probably
enough songs that had been wrote that you could sing
for the rest of your life and not ever done the same one
twice.

"That's so," Ursula said. "Variety is the spice of life."

"It sure is," I said.

She flicked her cigarette ashes on the floor and said,
"Wheeee, I've had lots of variety of the spicy kind."

"Have you traveled much?"

"One type of travelin. Not so much by rail, auto, or
airplane. Here, take another nippy-nip."

When I got through, she had herself some more
whisky.

I could tell we both was loosened up, so I said, "Come
on over here to the bed and set down by me."

She put on a record sang by a group of people about
this boy and gal that was gonna get married and their
parents wouldn't come to the wedding. They begged and
begged but the parents still wouldn't come.

As Ursula set down she said, "I wonder why parents
is so inconsiderate."

That made me think of her pa downstairs. "Your old
man won't be comin up here will he?"

"He won't come till I tell him to come. He's afraid
I'll go back to Manfred City. He has to buy me a purty
new present ever week."

I pulled Ursula over to me and we started to kiss.

"I bet he enjoys doin that," I said, "buyin you purty
things."

107

"He ain't got no choice."

We was laying back on the bed now and Ursula said, "I use to work in a pleasure house at Manfred City. That's where he got me. Him downstairs."

I didn't know what she was talking about but I said, "Did it give you pleasure?"

"Not much. Sometimes."

One thing led to another and we taken our pleasure for a good long time. When we was through and dressed we set a while on the side of the bed. I was running my hand through her hair and over her back.

"You're fabulous," she whispered to me.

"You're fabulous too," I told her.

The record player was going ba-zzz ba-zzz ba-zzz, and Ursula said she'd better take see to it.

"I got to go, Ursula." I stood up and stretched. "Is it any lipstick on me?"

She looked and told me no, and then she said she was gonna turn her back to me and not look at me again till I left. She told me it was because she liked me a lots.

At the door I said, "I sure thank you, Ursula, for bein so nice. Maybe I'll see you someday at Manfred City."

She answered with her back still to me. "Like as not. Ain't no tellin when I might leave here. I tell you what. If you need anything in Manfred City, like if you get down and out, you go to 188 Malburn Street and ask for Miss Delia and say that Ursula told you to go thar. Check in ever oncet and a while because I might be back."

I put the street and number and woman's name in my head so's I wouldn't forget.

We said good-bye and I went downstairs.

The owner was setting in a chair reading a newspaper. The other men had gone.

"Did you have a good time?" he asked me and had a grin on his face. I could tell by the sound of his voice that the grin didn't come out of no kindness.

"We listened to some Elvis records. One that was about a hound dog."

"Was the records fabulous?"

I said, "Yessir, they was good."

He got up and come over to where I was standing and held out his hand. "That'll be three dollars."

I looked him in the eye and seen that both of us knowed what the other was about. I pulled three dollars out of my pocket and give it to him.

"It oughta be five," he told me, "but I'll let you off with three."

As I was about to go out the screen door I said, "You shore have got a purty daughter."

He give me a look that would knock you down and he let out a sound that was like a laugh but wasn't one.

He said, "That goddam slut my daughter? I'd as soon the crows be peckin at my eyes. Miss Ursula is my wife."

He throwed down his paper to the floor and I went outside to head for Bessie.

Down the road the land begun to change, and now they wasn't fields and such but on both sides it was thick with tall pine trees. It was a lots cooler through here.

I still felt light from the whisky but I was beginning to get hungry.

I said to Bessie, "I wonder what time it is. We'll ride a little more and then I'll have Miss Mary Dove's lunch she fixed me."

I started to think about Ursula and the owner of the filling station, then put it out of my mind because I couldn't make head or tail of it. I decided I'd try to think on something that made sense to me. But didn't nothing make much sense to me that had happened recent except Miss Mary Dove and the fact that I liked Ursula a good bit—even if Ursula was that man's wife, which didn't seem likely, because of him letting me lay with her for one thing and because he was old enough to be my pa much less Ursula's who was younger than I was. Still, he didn't have no cause to lie to me about it.

Why, Ursula wasn't no more than a highly developed child, I said to myself, even if she did know lots about the body and so forth. Then I got to thinking that Ursula knowed a awful lot about the body, so I decided to put the whole thing out of my head again and sing one of the songs that we use to sing at Shady Grove. It was something about Heaven not being a airport but I couldn't remember all the words and give up on it.

"Here's a good place to turn off, Bessie." I pulled the right rein.

There was grazing for Bessie and it was cool for me. I laid down on my back on some pine needles and stretched my body. I was afraid I might go to sleep if I laid there long, so in a minute I sat up and opened the bucket that Miss Mary Dove had put my lunch in.

First thing off I seen a little radio that was either the one she played or the other one she'd talked about —I remembered she'd said she had two—and here she'd give one of them to me.

They was tucked beside it a piece of paper that I unfolded, and it said in ink:

Dear Rover Youngblood:

One radio is all I need and though I ain't a Commonist I would like to share with you and for you to
have this here radio. It might keep you company sometime when you haven't got nobody to talk to.

You can get the war news and they's a B'ham station that plays music all day long, some of it good.

You seem like a good boy and if the Lord is willing
I hope to see you again some time.

Yr. friend,

Mary Dove Truman

P.S. Here is the verse I have for listening to the radio.
I call it "Listening to the Radio."

If it's Sunday you can hear
Preachers shout from far and near.
If it's any other time
You can hear the latest crime.
Like as not you might feel blue.
Listen to a song or two.
Wars and rumors come and go
If you've got a radio.

M.D.T.

I didn't know what to think or say about that, Miss
Mary Dove doing such a kind deed as that, and her not
hardly knowing me and being afraid it might look like
she was a Commonist if she done such a thing and her
going ahead and doing it no matter.

I said out loud to myself, "Rover Youngblood, they
is some good people on this green earth and you ought to
be proud of it and love them fer it."

111

I answered back, "I know they is and I am proud and do love them fer it."

I flicked on the radio and started seeing what they was to eat. She'd put in a tomato wrapped in wax paper, a sausage sandwich, a apple, and three biscuits with jelly in them. It was all good.

I was too relaxed to move and thought I'd take me a short catnap. I'd cover some more ground before the sun started to set. I raked up a bunch of pine needles to put under my head for a pillow. I must of went to sleep the minute I laid my head down.

That's one thing I ain't never had trouble doing, is going to sleep. If I put my mind to it, and sometimes if I don't, I can drop off before you can snap your fingers. Ma wasn't never like that. She slept as light as a good hunting dog and she never did find it easy to drop off when she laid down. Pa could go to sleep all right and thunder couldn't wake him up when he did but he always was wide awake every morning when it was time for him to do his chores.

Chapter 11

WHEN I WAS WAKING UP it seemed like I was dreaming that me and Bessie was going up a high hill or mountain, not straight up it but around and around, and I knowed that when we got there everthing would be green and cool and just like you wanted it, but it seemed like everthing bad kept happening to keep us from getting there. For a while Bessie would slide down the hill, then I'd get her up to where we was at, then she'd slide down again. At one point somebody that looked like my ma would throw rocks at us to make Bessie run the other way, and when Bessie did sure enough there'd be the same somebody throwing more rocks at us to make Bessie run back right where we come from. We had a awful bad time of it and never did get to where we was going. We ended up by still being chased by rocks.

I ain't never been one much to dream and have probably not had enough experience along that line to put doubt as to the reading of dreams and thinking they can map out your future. I got my doubts even though my ma and pa both always put a lots of store to dreams. We had a nigger woman by name of Old Annie that lived out in the woods from Clearpoint in a little shack that didn't have but one room, with a dirt floor and straw on the dirt for her to sleep on. They was a kind of fireplace, and on the walls she had all manner of odd things such as dogs' skulls, snakes' skins, bugs and spiders pinned on a big piece of cardboard.

I never was there but oncet, and that was with ma and pa after ma'd had a dream that scared her. I wouldn't of went there by myself when I was little. Sometimes me and my two brothers would go in the woods close enough so's we could see the shack but we wouldn't go no closer. I'd heared she taken young boys and girls and cut them up to put in a snakebite remedy. I'd heared too that she chained you up and would put black widow spiders on you till they stung you to death.

This dream that ma had was about my brother Silas getting killed by being run over by a automobile. She worried and fretted around for three-four days till finally pa said, "You gonna waste yourself away if you keep on like this. We'll go to Old Annie's and see how she reads the dream." I begged them to take me along—and was afraid to go but at the same time wanted to.

Ma and pa got up a sack of fresh vegetables, some side meat, and some canned tomatoes to take to Old Annie. That's how you got her to give a good reading. If she didn't think you'd brought her enough, she'd just tell you a little bit to rouse up your curiosity and then

114

wouldn't say no more. That would be worse than not knowing nothing, so people would outdo theirselves to see that she had plenty.

Old Annie had a rag tied around her head, the way some of the gypsy women use to do that would come through Clearpoint. She and ma set at a old makeshift table, with pa beside ma and me beside him. Ma related her dream as to Silas getting killed, and said that she'd saw him laid out in the casket right there in our living room, with all the family passing by to take a final look.

Old Annie had inspected the sack of vegetables and so on right after we come in, so she knowed already how good a reading she would give. She taken a dog skull from the wall and put it on the table. Ma had to touch it and then she touched it and said some strange words over it.

Old Annie said, "Won't be no people dies. Be animule. Be before the next full moon."

That's all she said, wouldn't say no more, but it was enough for ma. She was comforted that it wasn't Silas or anybody else in the family that was fated.

Sure enough, before the new moon they was four of her laying hens that come up missing and a dog by the name of Spud that we'd had for seven years died on us. Ma and pa both was sure that these things was what Old Annie had read in the future.

I didn't get no conviction out of it because Spud was old enough to die and anything could of happened to them chickens—dogs, wild animals, or thiefs.

Well, I had been dreaming about me and Bessie trying to get to the top of the hill or mountain. When I got my eyes open good I thought I was still dreaming because right down at my feet was this little nigger girl standing there looking at me. She seemed to be about seven-eight year old.

I got myself up so's I was setting and said, "Howdy thar, Missy. What's yore name?"

She didn't let on but just stood without any kind of expression to her face. She was a nice-looking little girl with a blue dress on and one plait to her hair on top to the back of her head.

"My name is Rover Youngblood," I said. "I ain't going to hurt you." I don't know why I added the second part. She didn't look like she was afraid of me or nobody else.

"That hoss standin yonder is Bessie my mare. We are takin us a rest but on our way to Manfred City."

She set down on the pine needles. She had a paper sack full of something.

I told her, "I'll let you in on a secret if you'll tell me what yore name is and whur you come from and whur you goin."

She didn't say nothing at first but looked like her interest was up. Finally she said, "What kind of secret?"

"You got to promise me that if it's a good secret that you'll tell me what all I want to know."

She nodded her head that she would.

I put my hand in my overall pocket where my radio was at and turned the dial so it was on. It wasn't any time till some singer with a guitar come blasting out with a song about shooting his gal one Saturday night in a tavern.

The little girl just about went up in the air.

"Whut that?" she said.

116

"It ain't haints. And I'll tell you what it is jest as soon as you tell me what I want to know. You don't think I'm gonna set here and give you free information and you set there and not give me nothin, do you?"

She studied that over. She finally said, but like it was against her better judgment, "My name is Josephine Tucky White. I is called Tucky. I be babtized in the African Methodist Episcopal Church. I come from yonderways"—and she pointed to the woods—"and don't know whur I's goin."

"Tucky," I said, "I thank you. Looks like me and you is in the same shape. Leavin somewhurs and headin out to about near anywhurs."

I taken the radio out of my pocket and handed it to her. "It's a radio that don't have to be plugged in a wall. A old lady by name of Miss Mary Dove give it to me because she had two. It runs on batteries and you can get music, the war news, or anything you want. Like if I'm ridin along on my hoss over there, Bessie, and want to hear a song, I go right down the road in the middle of nowhur and listen to music. Now you can't beat that, can you?"

"Nawsuh."

I handed the radio to Tucky and showed her how to turn it on and get the different stations.

She landed on a preacher that was saying the end of the world would come before the year was out and that there wouldn't be over five hundred people living that could escape hell. He wanted everbody listening to send him a dollar bill to carry on with his work. He said the very dollar bill you sent him might be the thing that kept you out of fire and brimstone.

117

Tucky was smiling at the radio like it was about the finest thing she ever seen.

"See if you can get Manfred City," I said to Tucky. "Just turn that round thing around, slow, till you hear somebody mention Manfred City."

She did but nobody gave out the name. We ended up by listening to a report on the President and what him and his wife and daughters would be doing during the weekend. Seemed like he was going to be at a barbecue off in Texas and his wife was going to set and listen to music with people in Washington. The daughters was going off in two different directions but I can't remember what.

Tucky said, "It nice," and held right on to the radio.

"Have you eat today?" I asked her.

She told me she'd eat breakfast but that was all. I didn't have nothing left of the lunch Miss Mary Dove fixed me.

"You gonna get hungry before dark," I said.

"I's hongry now. I didn't eat but a biscuit with lard on it this mawnin."

"Tucky," I said, "you reckin you oughta run off from home like you're doin?"

She nodded yes.

"Well, you ain't very old. How old are you?"

"I's nine. I jes be nine. My birthday come on the lebenth of this month."

"Nine ain't much of a age to be goin out and takin on the world by yourself. Besides that, what's yore mammy gonna say when she finds you gone? She'll cry her eyeballs out. She'll think the KKK got ahold of you or that a rattler bit you or that you fell in a deep hole and

118

couldn't get out. Jest ain't no tellin what she'll think, and you bein a gal and not but nine year old. And what's worse about it, you bein a nigger gal."

"Say 'colored,'" Tucky said like she meant for sure for me to say it that way.

"All right, you bein a colored gal. It don't matter which way it is, nigger or colored, you got the same problems."

Tucky was looking down at her lap with a frown on her face, like she knowed as well as I did or better what all her problems was.

"Mama ain't gonna know I's gone. She awready be gone. Shoot."

"Whur's she at?" I asked.

"Don't know. Granny don't know. She runned off with Luke."

"Whur's yore daddy at then?"

She told me her daddy went off to the war before she was ever born and she hadn't ever saw him. She said she had five sisters and four brothers, all being took care of by her granny. Her granny hadn't been in no kind of a good humor since Tucky's mammy run off and she whupped the younguns about as much as she spoke to them. Everbody in the house went to bed hungry and like as not two-three of the younguns would go off to sleep bawling because their stomachs was empty.

By looking at Tucky I couldn't think of her ever crying in her whole life. She looked like the kind you couldn't pay to cry, not even if you was to put hot irons to the bottom of her feet. Her little brown eyes was set in her head so they looked like they'd witnessed about everthing both good and bad to see and that they wasn't

119

gonna be took advantage of by man, woman, or child. They come close to saying, but not all the way: I double-dog dare you.

"I's goin whur you're goin," Tucky said.

"Tucky, it's all I can do to take care of my own self and Bessie, much less a nine-year-old colored gal that is a runaway from home and might have the FBI lookin to find her."

She answered to that, "I wants to go with you."

"Aw, Tucky. Whur you belong's with yore granny. And yore brothers and sisters. Think how you gonna miss them."

All she said was, "Nawsuh."

I said, "Well, I reckin you can go with me to Manfred City but that don't mean I'm gonna take care of you for the rest of my life. When we get to Manfred City you gonna have to find a nice colored fambly to stay with. A preacher's fambly or somethin."

"I won't cause no trouble," Tucky said. Bless her heart, she had a smile on her face, about as big a smile as when she was looking at that radio that she was still holding. I thought to myself that she was like as not going to be holding that radio all the way to Manfred City.

"I don't know what we gonna do about you somethin to eat," I told her.

"I be awright," she said.

"That ain't the problem as to whur you'll be all right or not. The problem is you ain't got nothin in yore stomach and a youngun like you needs somethin to grow on. You don't want to be stunted, do you?"

She shaken her head that she didn't.

Right about then I heared a noise down the road and pretty soon seen a pickup truck coming along just fast enough to be moving. I thought to myself that whoever was driving wasn't going to get far if he kept on at that rate. Whoever it was was looking out to both sides of the road trying to spot something. Well, he spotted Bessie and Tucky and me, and stopped the pickup.

When he started coming toward us I seen it was that man from back at the filling station that had the long hair and didn't seem like he took to me much. He come slouching along with his hands in his pockets, mainly looking down at the ground.

When he got within about five foot of me and Tucky he said without a sign of a smile on his face, "Howdy. I thought you'd run off of the face of the earth."

I told him that no, I was taking my rest.

He squatted down and proceeded to pick up a pine needle and chew on it.

"What I wanted to see you about was this: I repasent the law through this part of the county, and when it's anybody that comes through on this road that don't live in this country, why, they have got to pay ten dollars to pass through. Since you ain't twenty-one year of age I'm gonna let you off by payin nine dollah and fifty cents. That thar's a bargain."

I knowed he was telling the biggest lie he could put together in his head. He'd made reference to my money when we was back at the filling station, and I didn't aim to let him have a cent of it.

"When did they take to chargin people fer goin through a county?" I asked him.

"In this state it's local," he said. "They don't do it in

121

ever county. This here one and two others that I know of."

"Well," I said, "what if you was to get in the county and you didn't have no nine dollars and fifty cents, much less ten dollars? What would happen to you then?"

"Have to throw you in jail." He spit out some pine needle. "Everbody is held by the law even if he don't know what the law is. It's Amurican. This here ain't no Commonist county. Hell's fire, if we was to let ever Commonist come through this county that wanted to and wanted to get off without what we charge to pass through the county, why, we'd be like Rusher, not believin in God, sleepin with the niggers"—and he give a look at Tucky—"and the whole face of Amurica would go to the dogs."

I couldn't tell for the life of me how he got off on all the business about the Communists and Russia and sleeping with niggers. It seemed like he was the kind that would get to rolling with his talk and run from one thing to another till he finally ended up with something that didn't have nothing to do with what he started out with. Anyhow, by way of his talk I could see he thought I didn't believe in God, not to speak of me being a Communist and sleeping with niggers.

"I ain't got no nine dollar and fifty cents to give you," I said. "If I did have, I wouldn't give it to you. They ain't no sech law as you said."

"You ain't callin me no liar, are you?" He squinted up his eyes.

"Ain't callin you nothin. Jest tellin you some things."

"You got awful big talk and britches not to be no older'n you air. You bein big enough to lay with Tullis'

122

wife don't make you big enough to take the law into yore own hands. Don't make you no man, neither. A hog can act by nature."

I reckoned he was referring to Ursula as being Tullis' wife.

"I ain't no hog," I said. "One thing more, I ain't givin you no money. Now or never. So's you might as well get in that pickup you like so much and would druther have than the Lord Jesus' convertible automobile and head out down the road. Me and Tucky don't want the likes of you."

His face kind of exploded like a fuse had been lit to it.

"Who do you think you talkin to, boy? I'd as soon to cut yore left ear off as to look at you. And as to that young nigger bitch settin there, I'd as soon she be boiled down fer makin lard. Hell's fire, boy, you and the nigger bitch ain't got no say-so around here. Around here we don't like Commonists and niggers and younguns like you that is tryin to upset the laws of the land. Hell's fire, boy, I ain't only gonna take the money but yore hoss there too. As fine fer resistin."

I said as easy as I could, because his talk wasn't putting me in the best of spirits, "You ain't takin my mare Bessie, now or ever more. If you got any law complaints bring me that sheriff that everybody was talkin about back at the filling station. I be willing to listen to him. Meantime, I don't want you referrin in no way to Tucky here or Bessie or the size of my britches. To begin with, this is overalls I am wearin."

I knowed he was not the kind that would fight fair. You can nearly always tell by the way a man talks, and I

don't mean by what he says but by the way he says it,
whether he would fight fair or not.

The man got up and walked to me and give me a right
smart kick on the leg. I jumped up. Out of his pocket
come a long knife that let a long mean-looking blade
spring out of it.

"Didn't count on this here, did you, boy?"

I wasn't in no mood to make talk with him.

We circled around some. I wanted us to get to circling
good, then for me to make a quick turn in the other
direction so's I could maybe get him from behind and
knock that knife out of his hand.

It didn't work thataway. He made a lunge at me and
the knife come close to putting a cut across the side of
my face. He was a little off balance so I heaved myself
at his ankles and throwed him. Someways or other we
ended up rolling on the ground till he was on top of me
and had that knife lifted above me, with me giving every
effort I had with one hand to hold the knife back and
my other hand was at his neck. I knowed if he got the
chance he was gonna kill me and that's all they was to
it. He wasn't hisself or nobody else's self but only what
he would of called a good Amurican fighting off a Commonist, which he would later on brag about to anybody
that would listen to him as to how he defended hisself
and all the pore innocent people of the county.

I pulled up all the strength I had in my body and give
a push, and at the same time tightened my hand on his
wrist that was leading to the knife. The knife dropped
to the ground. When it did, though, he clamped down
hard with both his hands on my throat and stuck his

thumbs right in. They wasn't no breath coming to me and I couldn't muster energy to fight him back.

Then, lo and behold, his hands relaxed and now I was fighting for nothing but to pull in as much air as I could. When I was back to being myself a little bit and could get some kind of notion what was going on, I seen he was laying on top of me and we was both bloody. I pulled myself out from under him and there sticking in his back was the long blade of that knife. Tucky was looking down at the knife like she was a bird and it was a snake and it had put a charm on her.

She said without no expression at all to her voice, "I's done pierced him three times."

She had him good and killed too. I pulled out the knife and turned him over. They was a little dirt across one cheek and his mouth hung open. The thing that come to my mind was, You gonna be needin a haircut fer all eternity, and even worse'n you do now, because yore hair's gonna grow some more before you rot.

"Yes, ma'am," I said to Tucky, "he is dead. What we got to do is get rid of that pickup truck and then to bury him."

All Tucky said was, "Yassuh."

I stuck the knife in the ground two-three times and then wiped it on some pine needles and stuck it in my pocket. Then I seen the blood on the side of my shirt and on my arms. I taken off the shirt right quick and wiped off my arms right quick. I got another shirt out of the sack I'd brought my clothes in.

"Tucky," I said, "we got to find a good place to bury

125

him. Where they won't be no animals pullin him out fer everbody to see."

Tucky had already been studying about that and she pointed to in back of us about thirty foot away where they was a clump of sassafras bushes. I got the man by his feet and drug him to the back of the bushes, out of sight. I put my bloody shirt with him.

"You stay right here and I'm gonna see what I can do with that there pickup truck," I told Tucky. "Stay hid if anybody comes by."

I went down to the pickup and the keys was in it. I hoped they was because I didn't want to go searching through that dead man's pockets.

I drove down the road about quarter of a mile without seeing nobody and then I noticed they was a opening to the woods and a hill. I taken the pickup in, went on up to the top of the hill, and seen that below it on the otherside they wasn't any houses that I could spot or a sign of human life, so I taken the truck out of gear and let it roll.

On the way back to Tucky I heared a automobile of some type off in the distance to the rear of me. I made a beeline off into the woods and throwed myself flat down on the ground till the automobile had passed on. I didn't have no notion what kind of a automobile it was because I didn't get my head up to look. I was hoping that Tucky was hid good.

To now, I hadn't thought no more about that dead man than if he'd been a catfish—I mean, about his not ever going to breathe again or take a gourd dipper of cool water from a well or to lay with a woman in a bed or anything it was that he enjoyed a lots. All I'd had

126

in mind was to get rid of him and his pickup so's to keep me and Tucky out of trouble. I didn't even *think* of it *that* way. It just come to me.

When I got back I didn't see Tucky anywhere. The spot where a man had got killed and where I had nearly got killed myself looked like it had been there forever without anybody even living on that spot much less dying on it. Tucky had fixed the pine needles where me and the man fought and where I drug his body.

"I's here," she said from back of the sassafras bushes.

When I got to her she was setting cross-legged and looking at the man's face in such a way that made you think she was trying to understand something about it, and whatever it was she wanted to understand wouldn't come to her.

They was a small rock on each one of his eyes.

"What them rocks doin there?" I said.

"To keep his eyes shet. He kep lookin and lookin at me. They to keep his eyes shet."

"He can't look at nothin, Tucky, out of them eyes. He may be lookin somewhurs into eternity but it ain't with them eyes. Them eyes has saw their last. We got to bury him."

Me and Tucky used rocks mainly and sometimes the knife to dig a place just deep enough to cover him over. It must of took us a good two hour and a lots of hard effort before we pulled him over and was ready to throw dirt on him.

"We got to say somethin before we cover him up," I told Tucky.

She said, "Yassuh."

I didn't know what to say because I didn't know

127

nothing about this man except for having met him two short times. Either one of these times I couldn't see nothing good about him but I knowed he must of did good things in his life.

I said, "Lord, if it's anybody to grieve when he don't show up, take care of them in their sorrow. Whatever sins he done, rest him of them. If you got a hell fer sech as us that are people, I hope he don't have to go to it."

I tried again to think of that song we'd sing at Shady Grove Church about Heaven not being a airport. This time the words come to me and I sung it low:

> Heaven ain't a airport
> Takin parcels in.
> You must shed yore body
> And yore mortal sin
> If you get to Heaven,
> If you get to Heaven
> A-bove.
>
> You can't use a parachute
> To ease you down to God.
> You can't pull a ripcord
> To land on that green sod
> When you're over Heaven,
> When you're over Heaven
> A-bove.
>
> If the Lord has blessed you
> Angels there will be
> Who will fly you over
> Life's tumultuous sea
> Till you get to Heaven,

Till you get to Heaven
A-bove.

Then I said, "Amen."

Tucky said, "I want's to say somethin." She bowed her head. "I is sorry I had to pierce this man with the knife three times. Ain't got nothin in perticler aginst him. It looked to be the onliest thing I could do. Name of Jesus. Amen."

I asked Tucky if she wanted to sing a song and she said mine would do for both of us.

I taken one last look at his face, that didn't look like no human face. The mouth hung down open so's you could see his teeth a little, and then there was the rocks on his eyes.

We throwed the dirt over him and packed it down, then covered it with pine needles, and taken the extra dirt off to scatter it here and yonder so's it wouldn't be noticed. Then we got some big rocks to put on the grave to keep off the animals. We done our best to make it look like nature or some man, woman, or child a long time ago had assembled those rocks together.

Tucky said, "I stick yore bloody sheert in he pocket."

"Thank ye, Tucky." I hadn't thought of that shirt one time while we was putting him to rest. If it was to come to me as my life job, I don't think I'd be much good at looking after corpses that I didn't want nobody to ever see again.

The sun was going down. You couldn't see it because of the pine trees but you could see over the tops of them a red-looking gold that seemed like it had tinfoil in it to make it sparkle so.

I wanted me and Tucky to get on off before night come. I didn't want to stay there with that man's body being inspected and thought about by the first bugs and worms that happened on to him. I wasn't afraid of nothing like a ghost or haint but afraid of the loss of the body which seems like all you've got to measure things by that you know about and like.

I looked to see if Tucky had the radio and she did.

"Come on, Tucky, let's be on our way. We might strike you up some food and if we don't do nothin else we'll be gettin closer to Manfred City. The onliest way we can lose out is by settin right here or walkin backward."

We both got on Bessie, with Tucky setting behind me. The grinding sound of Bessie's hoofs on the gravel road give me a feeling of the world being better off or at least a little more everday than it had been the last few hours.

Tucky said, "If they was to ketch me would I get lectercuted?"

"Ain't nobody gonna catch you."

"If they *was* to."

"Naw. They don't lectrocute younguns. They're innocent."

"I's *been,* and *seen.*"

"They don't know whur you been and whut you've seen. Remember all of the things you ain't seen, and one of the things you specially ain't seen, never, is that man we just buried. From right here on out I ain't never seen him but oncet in my life and that was earlier in the day at a filling station where we didn't have a bit of trouble except that I knowed he didn't like me."

Here was Tucky who at her age didn't have no calling to know how life got started much less to know how it ended, and who was a girl and colored besides that, well, here she was at age of nine year and had stabbed a man to death to save Rover Youngblood's precious skin.

I knowed she'd worry even if she didn't let on to it. She seemed like the kind that mulls over their griefs to theirselves and don't want to be disturbing nobody else.

I said, "Tucky, thank you fer savin me from that man. If it warn't fer you I'd be the one right now lookin into rocks fer guidance." I had to say that much, and I wasn't gonna dwell no more on what happened.

"Hit was did by nature," Tucky said.

The sky was coming to that time in the evening when it seems to get dark by jerks. The red-gold over the trees looked like somebody had built a fire under it and smoked it.

"You know what I'm gonna do when we get to Manfred City?"

Tucky waited a little bit before she answered. "Naw-suh."

"I'm gonna buy us a double-dip ice cream cone apiece. What is yore favorite kind of ice cream?"

"I never had but banella and never had that but twicet. Duke brough it to us."

"Well, there's lots of other kinds and you better start studyin right now so's you won't have to take too much time tryin to decide when you get to Manfred City. They's strawberry, choclit, and peach. Probly more."

Then it come to me. I thought to myself, Rover

Youngblood, you ain't got sense enough to pour ditch water out of a boot. Here's this youngun that ain't had nothin to eat all day but a biscuit with lard on it and you go on talkin about strawberry ice cream and sech, and you know if it was you and you was hearin this kind of talk yore tongue would be drippin water. What I'd tried to do was get her mind off one bad thing but all I'd did was to get it on another one.

"Tucky, turn on that radio and let's see what we can hear. Like as not we'll get somethin good at this time of the day."

A man come on who was advertising a funeral home. At first I thought it might be the funeral home of Miss Mary Dove's nephew but when they give the name of the town it wasn't Manfred City but a place I'd never heared of called Suckling. When the man was through advertising about how permanent the caskets was and how we all wanted our loved ones to stay just like God made them, some mournful music started playing and the same man started telling who-all had died for the past few days, what was wrong with them, who they was survived by, and when and where they was going to be buried.

All the talk about death and burying wasn't making me feel no better. I told Tucky she could turn to any station she wanted to. She kept it right there for the whole fifteen minutes.

Now it was dark, not bold dark but at that time when it looks like a thin dark cloth has been dropped over everthing. Lightning bugs had started to streak around, and night noises from the woods commenced.

"Tucky, you ever heared of the ɪɪɪᴜɴ? Some kind of a men's club?"

"Yassuh. They been at our quarters a lots of times. They mean."

"Whatta they do?"

"Bad."

Tucky had the radio turned down low with music coming from it. Gospel singing.

"You ain't tellin me nothin when you jest tell me they're bad. That ain't no kind of a answer."

"One time they got on Bubba Washington that lives next to me. They come up in the night, on they hosses, and they pitched rocks at Bubba's doah. They all weared sheets.

" 'Bubba!' they hollered. 'Come on out, Bubba Washington!' He be asleep. Somebody pitch a big rock through Bubba's windah and he get up and come to the poach. He woman Maybelle stand behind him with they baby and with Spud give to her by Duke.

"The mans on hosses say, 'Got a new woman, Bubba?' He say, 'Yassuh.' 'You don't keep one long,' they say. He say, 'Nawsuh.' They all laugh and Bubba he try to act like it be funny to him too.

"One time Bubba work a year at *De*troit and the mans say, 'Why ain't you went back up yondah to the Yankeedoodles?' Bubba say he like it where he at.

"One man holler, 'Come on, Bubba, and do us some runnin. Bet you ain't had no exacise today.'

"They put a rope around Bubba's middle and run him up and down the road with they hosses trottin. Bubba holler at them, 'Genelmans, I ain't got no shoes on my feets and these rocks they hurt!' One man holler to him, 'Thought you had hoofs, Bubba.'

"Bubba's feets was bad. Granny binded them when the mans was gone.

"Bubba he cryin and say, 'I know them whites. I know them to the last one. They all from Sycamore, Alabama. I's gonna get them. I's gonna get Mr. Rayburn Phillips who it was that held that rope. I's gonna have white blood on my hands someday. I's gonna carve the bottoms they feets with a knife.'

"Bubba still be cryin. Maybelle she cryin and the baby cryin. Spud he be jes lookin.

"Granny say, 'Hesh yore tawk, Bubba. You ain't gonna do nothin. Nawsuh. You ain't gonna do nothin.'

"Bubba cry and say, 'I is. I is. I is.' "

Tucky hushed and we rode on hearing the gospel singers.

Finally I said, "Why was it they run him like that?"

"They likes to."

"Had Bubba did somethin bad?"

"He runned off to *De*troit and wuk."

"Don't sound like them men got much to do or study about," I said to myself more than to Tucky. I thought to myself that if pa was to stay up half the night or more running niggers up and down the road he wouldn't never be able to get up in the morning to do his chores, much less to plant his crops and bring them in. Men such as the iiiun must of been rich or else had somebody else to take care of them and their families.

Even if I was rich, I thought to myself, I'd a heap ruther do somethin else than run niggers up and down the road in the middle of the night.

I could make out up ahead of us a sign but it was dark enough that I couldn't read it yet. I hoped it would say something good and by hoping that, I didn't have no idea what it was I wanted. It turned out to be good anyhow because when we was up close enough that I could read the sign it said: BENNETT'S SOUVENIRS, 2 MI., SUCKLING, ALA., 1,218 POP., SEE BENNETT INDIAN CAVE.

"Tucky," I said, "looks like we can get you somethin to eat. What we'll do is, when we get to Suckling we'll get you somethin to eat and then on the other side of Suckling when we get off a piece from town we'll look fer a good place to stop by the side of the road and sleep. How you like that?"

She said, "Awright. But I's got to be keerful. They's the HUN at Suckling. Flora one time she wuk fer a white woman at Suckling. I hear Flora tawk to my granny. She say she couldn't be on the street without the white woman be with her."

"Well, you're with me," I said. "If anybody bothers us I'll say that I got a old maid aunt by name of Miss Dove Yancey that lives at Manfred City and that yore sister cooked fer her till she got the mumps and died, so Miss Dove sent off fer you because you come from a whole fambly of good cooks that has been workin fer the Yancey fambly since way back before the Civil War. I'll say Miss Dove's fambly is one of the oldest in this part of Alabama. I'll say that if it's anybody that wants to bother you they better study about tanglin with Miss Dove because Miss Dove Yancey don't care nothin about the po white trash that is Yankees to begin with and come here after the Civil War to take advantage

135

of the South both black and white. If it's anybody that bothers us, Tucky, you let me tell my story and don't say nothin. I'll say that you're deef and dumb."

It must of been all right with Tucky. She didn't say nothing.

Tucky had a serious way about her that reminded me of my brother Silas. Except when you looked at Tucky, and that would be off at a distance, you wouldn't never think she was just nine year old. When you got up close to her and seen her face and especially her eyes, she looked a lots older than nine year. She didn't carry on with no foolishness.

Brother Silas, younger than both me and Ed and the one you'd think was gonna carry on with foolishness, always done his chores the way they was suppose to be done, saved his money, carried on growed-up conversations with his schoolteacher, and the like. The only thing, his face looked more like a youngun's than Tucky's did.

"Looky yondah!" Tucky said.

I had already saw it. They was colors of pink and blue in the darkness. I knowed it was some part of the town of Bennett but I didn't know what.

"It looks like somebody's usin up a lots of lectricity," I said.

Shore enough they was, because when we got to where the pink and blue come from we seen this big barn-looking building but the size of two-three barns and several signs made up of pink and blue lights that said: THE TOP HAT, BUDWEISER BEER, DANCING, COME IN, WELCOME.

136

About seven cars and pickups was out front in a parking lot.

I said to Tucky, "Let's stop right here and go off into this field. You and Bessie can wait fer me while I go and try to buy you some samitches. I don't reckin they allow colored folks."

Tucky said it was all right with her because she wanted to lay down and rest a little bit. "Don't make no haste," she said. "I's tard."

As I got closer to the Top Hat I heared music playing. When I walked inside, the music was turned on so loud that it hurt my ears. It was dancing music.

The front part of the Top Hat was the place where they sold beer, food, and so forth, and it wasn't very big compared to the back part where I seen tables and chairs and people dancing.

They was three-four people setting on stools at the counter so I decided to set down too and have me a beer. Tucky had told me she was tired and not to hurry none, and I wanted to see what all of this activity was.

The man behind the counter was short and right fat, especially at the face and belly. He had thick lips and a cigarette hanging out of them to the side.

"Whut can I do fer you?"

"Gimme a beer," I said.

He wanted to know what kind.

"Hit don't matter," I told him. "Whatever you drink."

I never had drank but a few beers because beer wasn't legal at Clearpoint and so I didn't know all the different names.

137

What he brought me was the kind I'd saw advertised outside, Budweiser beer. He set down a glass for me to pour it in.

They must of been going on thirty-forty signs covering the four walls of that front room. For instance, over this wide door that went into where the people was dancing I seen a lots of signs and the biggest said, DANCING. Then they was other signs, not so big, around it: NO OVERALLS ON THE DANCE FLOOR, NO LADIES IN SLACKS OR SHORTS ON THE DANCE FLOOR, NO LOUD OR PROFANE LANGUAGE ON THE DANCE FLOOR, NO HARD LIQUOR ON THE DANCE FLOOR. I wouldn't of been a bit surprised if they'd had a sign that said, NO DANCING ON THE DANCE FLOOR, but they didn't.

The waiter come back down the counter for me to pay him.

"How much?" I said.

"Quarter. Thirty-five on the dance floor."

I thought, I could set here and tap my feet to the music and save a dime per beer.

About four-five stools down from me they was a man setting who was talking to hisself. I couldn't tell what he was saying. He had a bigger than ordinary nose, was brown-looking, and he didn't seem to be a pure American. He had awful black hair with a good deal of grease put on it.

I didn't mean to be staring at him but I guess I was. He must of caught me out of the side of his eye because he turned around to me and said, "Boy, what're you looking at?"

I said, "I was lookin at a bug that was flyin past

you. I thought at first it was a hornet but it warnt. I
was afraid it might sting you."

That seemed to satisfy him because he picked up his
bottle of beer and moved down next to me. He was big
with lots of muscles and the flowered shirt he had on
was so tight it pulled at the buttons and it looked like
they might pop off. He had a scar across the left side
of his face and one on his left arm.

"I don't like no hornets," he said. "Or no wasps."

I agreed with him that I didn't either.

He proceeded to tell me how one time he got stung
by four hornets one after another and he swole up so
bad that his eyes closed shut. I told him how a bee had
stung me inside my ear. We give stories back and forth
such as these and I ended up by telling how brother Ed
had got a wasp down his overalls and was stung on the
privates. Me and the man got a big laugh out of that,
but I remembered that brother Ed didn't get no laugh,
and what made it worse was that I'd ask him in front
of people where did he get stung, and Lamour Anne
and Naomi would snicker ever time he come in a room.
Ma put a end to that by not giving us no sweets for
three days.

The man told me, "My name is Hiwasse."

I didn't know if that was his first or last name.

I said, "My name is Rover Youngblood."

He taken a long drink out of his beer bottle. "I ain't
never seen you around Bennett."

"I ain't never been to Bennett. I come from Clearpoint."

The name of Clearpoint didn't seem to strike no bell

with him. On the other hand, he knowed all about places like Mobile, Birmingham, Montgomery, Florence, not to mention towns in other states that he talked about.

The conversation led from one thing to another till he finally told me he was a pure-blooded Cherokee Indian. I could of fell off of the stool because on two sides of my family I had a little Cherokee blood myself. Pa never did let on about it because he wasn't proud of it but ma was and I was. In school when we studied the Indians the teacher would always say there was a part Indian setting in the very room. It always made me proud when everbody would turn around to look at me. At recess the younguns would come up and say, "What does it feel like to be a Indian?" or "Did yore ancestors do much scalpin?" or "Can you shoot with a bow and arrow?"

Hiwasse told me that people called him Hi.

I said, "Hi, I'm part Cherokee on two sides of my fambly. The Youngbloods come from Georgia."

That made Hi so happy that he ordered us both another beer and he wouldn't let me pay for my own.

He held up his beer in the air and said, "Here's to a full-blooded Cherokee and a half-assed Cherokee." Then he let out a big laugh and whopped me across the back.

"Don't you live on a reservation or somewheres like that?" I asked Hiwasse.

"Nah. I got a old woman and three kids and they stay wherever I put'm at. I keep movin about, with carnivals, rodeo, labor jobs, whatever is there when I get ready for it."

140

Hiwasse had a way of talking that was different from most that I'd ever heared. He didn't sound like a foreigner but then he didn't sound like no white folks from around Clearpoint and for sure not like no niggers. It seemed like he give more to a word than most of the people I'd knowed.

The Top Hat was beginning to fill up with people. I started to think about Tucky and her food, and her and Bessie out in the field.

"I gotta be goin purty soon," I told Hiwasse.

"Nah. It's early. It ain't but Cherokee women goes to bed early. Along with the babies." He said to the waiter, "Bring me and this boy another beer, Eddie."

He's gonna get you drunk, I told myself, and this ain't no time or place for getting drunk.

I told Hiwasse that it wasn't that I was going to bed right away but that I had things to do before I could go to bed. I said, "I got lots to take keer of."

"Like what?" he wanted to know.

I give him a quick history of me running away from home, what had happened to me along the way and who I'd met, and I told him that Tucky and Bessie was waiting for me but I knowed that Tucky was asleep. I didn't tell him about Tucky killing the man.

Hiwasse said that every boy had to go off on his own. He said he'd expect it from his three younguns when they got up old enough. "I shined shoes in New Orleans," he said, "a long time before I was as old as you are. I ain't got no recollection of my old man."

Hiwasse seemed awful happy and smiled and laughed out loud a lot. I didn't know if he was drunk or getting drunk or if maybe this was just his normal way.

141

I noticed that men was going to the dance floor with overalls on and paying no attention to the sign that said not to.

"Hi, how come they don't allow no overalls on the dance floor?"

He said it was because they wanted folks to be more dressed up.

That didn't make no sense to me, because I'd been wearing a clean pair of overalls to church ever since I could remember. It was what ma give me to wear and ma was as strict as anybody on earth about wearing the right thing when you was suppose to and it being clean. Most of the people going to the dance floor, whether they had on overalls or what, didn't look very clean. I thought to myself that I couldn't say much about cleanliness right then because I hadn't as much as sponged off my body since I left Clearpoint.

Me and Hiwasse had to talk loud to each other because the music was so strong and the place had filled up with so many people. Somebody was setting at every stool at the counter.

Hiwasse started to tell me a story about when he was a pimp in Mobile. I didn't have no notion what a pimp was and told him so. That like to of tickled him to death and he nearly fell off of the stool he laughed so hard. Even after he had explained it to me, I couldn't see what was so funny about me not knowing the word. I thought to myself that they was probably lots of words that Hiwasse didn't know.

I tried to come up with such a word and then remembered "procrastinate," that we had learned to spell

142

at school and had to use in five different sentences.

"What does 'procrastinate' mean?" I asked him. I spelled it out.

Sure enough, he didn't know what it meant, and that cooled him off from laughing so much. He said the word over four-five times like he aimed to remember it.

"I can't drink no more beer," I told Hiwasse, "because if I do I won't feel like nothin tomorrow, and I got a mare and a nigger youngun to take care of."

"A Cherokee even if he's half-ass don't let beer bother him none. I got some whiskey outdoors at my motor scooter. You oughta see my motor scooter. I won it shootin craps and it's red."

He had to tell me what a motor scooter was and also what craps was. If he was to laugh at me for not knowing what they was, I had two more hard words in my head that we learned to spell at school, and I was going to pull them on him. He might of figured I was gonna do that because he didn't laugh. All he done was smile a little.

The motor scooter taken my interest, and I thought to myself that it was the same color as the Lord Jesus Turner's convertible. Then that got me to wondering where the Lord Jesus was at and if he was looking for me and his nail. I put my hand into my pocket to see if the nail was still there, which it was.

A girl wearing a print dress and with a good bit of paint on her face come up between me and Hiwasse and said, "Hi, Hi," because "Hi" was Hiwasse's nickname. Then she giggled. She had a bottle of beer in her hand.

Hiwasse give her a light spank on the rump and told her my name was Rover. I don't think he knowed her name and if he did he didn't say it.

She said, "Red Rover, Red Rover, let Ollie May come over. That's my name, Ollie May." She laughed big enough so's I could see a cavity in the back of her mouth. She was a right purty gal when she kept her mouth fairly closed.

Ollie May said, "Why don't one of y'all buy me a beer?"

Hiwasse told her how broke him and me was and that he was having to charge all of his beers till he got paid the next day.

While he was going on with all of that, a man about six foot tall, wearing a undershirt, and with five-six tattoos on his arms, come up to Ollie May and pulled her by the arm.

"Bitch woman," he said, "get back yonder to yore table."

He give her a shove, and he give me and Hiwasse a ugly look.

Ollie May called him a dirty name and said to us in a singsong voice, "See you, boys." Then the two of them went to the dance floor room.

"That gal'll cause a fight before the night's over," Hiwasse said and seemed like he thought it was a good idea.

I told him I had to go relieve myself, and he said to go outdoors, around to the side of the building. When I got there, they was man and woman alike relieving theirselves and talking to one another like they wasn't nothing unusual about it. I went off behind a clump of bushes, where it was dark.

When I got back inside I told Hiwasse about it and he said we wasn't in no high-class place. "These here is po white trash," he told me. "They ain't got no Cherokee blood like you and me."

I didn't see what Cherokee blood had to do with it but I could tell we was among the po white trash. One woman was doing a dance with her skirt pulled up over her head and a man setting on a stool was throwing peanuts at her bloomers. Such as that went on and people didn't seem to think much about it. My ma and pa would of dropped dead.

I started to tell Hiwasse what all it was I wanted to do when I got to Manfred City or wherever I finally ended up. I said I'd like to get a steady job and buy a suit of clothes, take a ride on a airplane, buy some whisky like Ursula had give me, send some nice presents to all the members of my family and to Miss Mary Dove Truman, get all the poontang I wanted, and so forth. I went on and on, and most of it was beer talk.

Hiwasse said they wasn't no need for me not to have any of them things. He said he'd had just about all of them.

"When I was with the rodeo I rode in a airplane all the way to Arizona and back," he told me. Then he said, "I think I'll go to Manfred City with you and the nigger gal. I'm gettin tired of this here place."

I asked him, "What about yore wife and younguns?"

He said they was took care of there in Bennett and he'd come back to get them when he taken a notion.

"They won't run off and leave me," he said and laughed.

I thought, Me and a full-blooded Cherokee and a nigger youngun and no telling what else all trying to get to Manfred City. But I was glad for Hiwasse to come along because I liked him and it seemed like we was kin to each other, with both of us having the same blood.

Right about then the gal that called herself Ollie May come back to talk to us.

"Your sweetheart ain't gonna like it with you standin here," Hiwasse told her. Hiwasse didn't seem to care one way or another.

Ollie May said, "He's my old man and I ain't slep with him fer a month. Hit don't matter what that son-ofabitch likes. *I* like *you*. And *him*." She give me a thump on the shoulder and giggled.

I told her, "Thank ye," and said that I thought she was purty.

She wanted to know, "Do you *ril*ly or are you jes kiddin me?"

I told her I wouldn't of said it if I didn't mean it.

She wanted to know if Hiwasse thought she was purty.

He said if you didn't care what you called purty he guessed she was purty, but he winked at her to show that he didn't mean no offense and she seemed to take it all right.

She was telling us how she liked the song that was playing that was called "One Broken Heart on the Rocks," when all of a sudden from I don't know where, come up her husband and whammed her across the face with the flat of his hand so that she went sailing across the room.

"What air you doin makin up to my wife, you son-

146

ofabitch?" he said to Hiwasse. His face was splotched red and they was sweat at his neck and at the armpits of his undershirt.

"Don't know whatcha mean," Hiwasse said. "She was asking me about a girl friend of hers that's my cousin. My cousin has got pneumonia and is about to die."

"Yeah?" The husband looked like maybe he believed Hiwasse and that maybe he had did the wrong thing.

People was gathering up around us. Ollie May was across the room and jumping up and down to beat sixty she was so mad. She started to come after her husband but two men held her back.

"I want part of his nose!" she hollered. "I want part of the sonofabitch's ear! Lemme go! Lemme go!"

Hiwasse went on as calm as could be, telling how Ollie May and his cousin went to school together, got up their lessons together. He ambled on, as easy as you please, and then taken up his beer bottle like he was going to have him a swaller, but instead he drawed back the bottle so quick you couldn't even think about it and brought it across the side of the husband's head. The husband sunk to the floor, but in his place they come up several of his friends that was all over me and Hiwasse. The waiter behind the counter was working at them, over us. Right soon it was a free-for-all and Hiwasse dropped down to the floor by his stool and pulled me down.

"Ain't no sense in bein up there," he said to me. "Ain't it nice down here?"

I told him it was a sight better down here than it was up there.

"Ollie May's husband ain't no count," he said. *"I've*

147

seen him ridin around with his sheet on. He don't like Indians cause he ain't one."

"Is he a Klu Kluxer?"

"Nah, he's a ᴍᴜɴ. He can't even have a tavern fight without all his buddies with him. One full-blooded Cherokee and one half-ass can take care of his whole works." Hiwasse laughed.

Above us they was still storming. I could hear glass breaking and chairs thundering, a awful lot of cussing did by the men, and women squealing. Around Hiwasse and me all we could see was legs and shoes. Ever now and then I got a glance at Ollie May's husband's face, about three foot away, and he was still knocked out. His buddies that had come up to help him out was doing him more harm than good because he was getting stepped on all over and bloodied up in general. If he done any night riding with the ᴍᴜɴ it was gonna have to be by way of a wheelchair.

"Looka here," Hiwasse said. Right beside us they was a man's foot and leg and the pants was rolled up about six inches. The man's leg was thick with hair, and so Hiwasse taken a match and lit it.

"If he was a good Indian he wouldn't have so much hair on him like that," Hiwasse said.

The man started stomping his foot the best he could but evidently was so busy with what he was doing up above us that he couldn't get down to see what was happening below.

"Start crawlin down toward the end of the bar," Hiwasse told me. "I'll follow you."

So we struck out, easing along like two bears. When we got to the end and stood up, nobody paid any attention to us. Everbody, women alike, was matched up with somebody else and scrapping every way they could, from punching to hair pulling and biting. I didn't glimpse Ollie May.

They wasn't nobody in the dance floor room, and Hiwasse said for us to go in there.

"The cops'll be here in a minute," he said. "We can go through the kitchen and out the back."

Then he said, "Wait a minute." He went to the record player and put his hand in the back of it to turn the thing up so loud it sounded like the whole building was shaking from the noise. I couldn't even tell what the song was about.

"Ain't that purty?" Hiwasse said and smiled like he had just fathered a youngun.

We went into the kitchen that wasn't much size at all. If anybody had been working back there they wasn't there now. On a wood table I seen two loafs of bread, a pork roast, and some tomatoes. My first thought was that I was hungry. Next I remembered I'd promised to get Tucky some food.

I started to explain it to Hiwasse but he was pulling a sack of eggs out of the icebox.

"Grab some eggs," he told me.

They was a cut through the wall about two foot high and several foot long, so that whoever was working in the kitchen could hand food and such to the waiter outside behind the counter. Hiwasse started sailing eggs through there and by time a egg had splattered across somebody's face he'd be ducked down. The people didn't have no notion where the eggs was coming from and didn't have time to try and find out.

I started sailing eggs too, till we heared a siren and then heared somebody trying to get in the back door of the kitchen.

The screen was latched and a man hollered, "Open up! Name of the law!"

Hiwasse told me to open the door and act like I worked in the kitchen. He grabbed a dishrag and started rubbing on a pan.

These three men in blue uniforms and pistols in their hands come rushing in like they'd as soon shot the Queen of England as look at her.

"What's agoin on hyar?" the tallest and skinniest one said. They was all three tall and skinny, and they could of been brothers.

"I don't know except we've got us a fight out there. Here I was tryin to make up a order of pork samitches when all of a sudden—"

The tallest one cut me off when he seen Hiwasse. "What're you doin in here, Hiwasse?"

"Me and this boy started workin today in the kitchen. It don't pay much but—"

The policemen headed for the door, like they didn't have time to stand there and listen to us talk about our jobs.

"Officer!" Hiwasse called.

They all three stopped, and he said, "I seen the whole thing start from right here. It was Willie Joe Crawford that started it. Him and his niun buddies. Willie Joe hit his wife Ollie May and then all the niun boys come to Willie Joe's rescue. It was a sight, all of them men ganged against one woman."

150

The policemen didn't stay to hear no more.

"Let's get," Hiwasse said.

"I got to take Tucky some food."

We hustled about and put a big chunk of pork, a loaf of bread, and three nice ripe tomatoes in a paper sack. Then I thought at the last minute to get three Coca-Colas and pull them. I put fifty cents in change on the table.

"What's that for?" Hiwasse asked me.

"It's to pay fer this here food."

"You ain't tryin to kid me?" he said and let out a big laugh.

I told him, "I shore ain't tryin to kid you. I'm payin fer this here food like I told you I was."

"Let's get outa here anyways," he said and we made it out the back door.

He told me that his motor scooter was over by some oak trees and for me to go on to the edge of the field and wait for him.

I jogged along, not really running because I didn't want to spill the Coca-Cola. All the racket that was coming out of the Top Hat made you think that the roof might all of a sudden go sailing up in the sky.

I got to the edge of the field and it wasn't no time till Hiwasse come bouncing along, making a prrrattt-prrrattt noise.

"Hop on," he said. I did and guided him to where Tucky and Bessie was.

I could see Tucky good enough by the moonlight to tell she had a big rock drawed back over her shoulder and was ready to let it fly. I couldn't blame her, with

151

that motor scooter and all its racket and two unknown figures coming roaring at her in the night and her asleep.

"Tucky! It's me, Rover! Put down that there rock. I gotcha somethin to eat."

Hiwasse shut down his scooter and we got off. Bessie seemed relieved. She'd been making some squealing noises at the scooter.

"Tucky, I'd like fer you to meet my friend Hiwasse, a full-blooded Cherokee. I'm part Cherokee too. And Hiwasse, I'd like fer you to meet Tucky, a full-blooded colored person and somebody that I owe a lots to."

They shaken hands.

"That there, Hiwasse, is my mare Bessie." I give Bessie a pat on the flank.

Then I told Hiwasse that me and Tucky was tired and wanted to find us a place to lay down for the night, and that for several reasons we'd just as soon not be run up on by strangers or anybody else.

Hiwasse said, "I know a good patch of woods the other side of Bennett. Don't nobody go there because it's near the Indian mounds and folks say they're hainted. Lemme see." He stopped for a minute. "We better not go by this here front road. It's gonna be hot with policemen and the iiiun and there's gonna be some folks includin Willie Joe Crawford, if his face ain't ground into the floor, that won't have no love for me.

"But they's a back road. We can go right through this field, hit on the back road, miss Bennett entarly, cut back to the front road, go a little ways, and then there we are at the woods."

152

Me and Tucky got on Bessie, and Hiwasse started up his scooter.

"I'll head right straight through yonder," he said and pointed, "and wait on you at the road. This motor scooter won't go slow enough for you on that there hoss. Be seein you."

Off he taken, going prrrattt-prrrattt.

We didn't go in no hurry because Bessie had to kind of feel her way along. They was holes and such, even if Hiwasse didn't seem to pay them no mind. I figured it would be a lots bigger loss to have Bessie hurt than it would to have that scooter hurt.

Tucky was holding on to my waist. Up to now she'd been quiet.

"I don't wanta be whur they's haints," she said.

"What air you talkin about, Tucky?"

"Haints," she said. "Whur them Indians is buried."

"They ain't no haints. It's the livin to be lookin out fer."

"I got one haint."

"Whata you mean you got one haint?"

"That man's. That I kilt." Tucky's voice was low and like it wasn't coming from a person but just from somewhere in the dark.

"Tucky, that man hasn't got no haint. One thing, his body lays back yonder whur we put it under them rocks. Them rocks ain't moved and his haint ain't lifted through them. Next thing, we done our best to pray his soul to Heaven. That was the best we could do. If he didn't get there, then it was ordained that he go some-whurs else. Last, it wasn't yore fault that you kilt him

153

but out of self-defense fer me and finally self-defense fer yoreself because he'd of kilt you when he got through with me. Now, study it thataway."

Tucky said she'd try to.

"Turn on the radio," I said.

The announcer said that he was about to play the three top tunes of the week and that every one of them had came from England. He said it looked like the folks in the United States of America could come up with their own songs but that we still hadn't got weaned off of England yet. Song number three was called "Turn Me Over," which was repeated throughout the song except when the singers would say every now and then, "I'm too hot hot on this side." It wasn't much of a song but it had a good rhythm to it. I could tell it was helping Tucky with her haint because she had commenced to hum with the music.

As to haints, I told Tucky I didn't believe in them but I didn't know if I believed in them or not. I mainly just didn't study about them. If I was to see one standing in front of me I'd say, "There is a haint." Up to that time I'd try to have my mind on something else. Of course I didn't want Tucky to think there even might be such a thing.

We didn't miss Hiwasse over fifty foot when we got to the road.

"Just follow me," he said. "I'll ride up a ways and wait on you, and then I'll ride up a ways more."

We done this till we'd got clear around to the front road and come to where the woods was.

Hiwasse said, "I'll roll this here scooter through the woods."

154

Me and Tucky got down off of Bessie so's I could lead her. Tucky grabbed my free hand and held it tight.

Hiwasse made his way ahead of us, cussing at the bushes and briars and wanting to know why the hell it was so dark.

I said to Tucky, "Even if they was any haints here, which they are not, they wouldn't hurt us none because Hiwasse is a full-blooded Indian, I'm a part, and you're colored. They'd like as not be good spirits to us."

Tucky didn't let go.

In front of us Hiwasse said, "Here's the clearin to where the mounds begin. We might as well stop right here."

I put down the sack of food that also had in it the Coca-Colas and then hitched up Bessie to the bush or young tree, I couldn't tell which. Hiwasse done something with his scooter. Tucky stayed about one inch from me ever step I taken.

Finally all of us got together and set down, and then I opened up the sack. Before I thought of it good I started to take the knife out of my pocket so's I could cut the roast and tomatoes, and then I thought, Oh Lord, it's the one Tucky killed the man with.

I said, "Hiwasse, have you got a knife so's I can make some samitches?"

He said, "Yes," and handed me one of these here thick knives that has three-four blades in addition to opener, corkscrew, and everything else you can think of.

I handed Tucky the first sandwich and after she'd thanked me she lit into it like she was half starved, which I guess she nearly was.

155

Hiwasse said he didn't mind if he had one.

Me and Tucky had us a Coca-Cola each but Hiwasse said he guessed he'd have some of his whisky and wanted to know if I didn't want some too. I told him I'd be much obliged after I got done eating.

"I hope they fill up the jailhouse tonight," Hiwasse said and laughed big. "They can have a meetin of the IIIUN and elect officers. If Willie Joe Crawford is still alive and breathin, maybe they'll make him president. I'd like to get me some of his wife, though.

I said, "Hiwasse, we got a child settin here."

He asked Tucky to excuse him and said he'd talked bad for so long and been around so many bad-talking women, not to mention bad-talking men, that he'd got to where he wouldn't remember when he was around younguns and ladies.

"It's like smokin cigarettes," he said, "a habit." Then he offered me a cigarette and I told him I didn't smoke.

"Don't you do nothin bad?" he wanted to know. "You ain't even a half-ass Cherokee—excuse me, Miss Tucky—if you don't do *nothin* bad."

I told him I done a lots of bad things but that ever since I'd made a bet with Edgar Partew that I could chew a wad of tobacco longer than he could without spitting, I'd not have no crave for tobacco in any form. I told him that I did win the bet but that I couldn't hold nothing on my stomach for two-three days afterward.

"It's a bad habit," Hiwasse said, "but it satisfies me. All my bad habits satisfies me."

He handed me the whisky bottle and the three of us set there for a while, me and Hiwasse drinking, not saying nothing. Tucky had cut off the radio when we commenced to eat, because I told her she might wear out the battery. I think she would of like to let it stay on all the time.

Hiwasse said after a while, "I don't know why it is I like to fight so much."

I told him I could take it or leave it.

He went on, "With me it's next best thing after a woman. No, third best thing. Whisky comes second. Might as well say second and third because whisky and fightin comes together. After I been fightin I feel relaxed and good, like I do now."

That was the first time that Hiwasse wasn't laughing and carrying on, so I figured he meant what he was saying to me.

I told him I knowed the feeling but that I didn't get it from fighting.

Tucky started yawning which turned around to set me to yawning. When I thought for a minute of all that had happened during that day it seemed like it could of been a year: Miss Mary Dove and husband, Ursula, Tucky and a killing, Hiwasse and a fight, and now going to sleep at the Indian mounds.

I'd had enough alcohol put into me during the day to have made me mean and roaring, but I figured that because so much had happened my mind had stayed clear.

"I'm gonna go to sleep," I told Tucky and Hiwasse.

Tucky took to that notion and laid right down. I give her my sack of clothes for a pillow.

"I can take some rest," Hiwasse said. "I ain't done nothin to speak of all day but I can take some rest."

I stretched out and begun to wonder how my family was doing. I knowed they'd probably been in bed for a long time. At least ma and pa had. I wondered if they was grieving over me.

Then I went to sleep.

When I woke up it was pitch black and I knowed that something had woke me up but I couldn't understand what. It seemed like it had been some kind of a sound. Hiwasse was snoring away but that wouldn't of woke me. Then all of a sudden Tucky, right beside me, let out a little holler from her sleep and then moaned some. Then she set straight up and grabbed for me.

"What's the matter, Tucky?"

She was shaking and a odd sound was coming from her throat, like maybe she couldn't get her breath good.

"Hit were his haint after me," Tucky said.

"Whose?"

"The man I kilt. And he were a Indian with feathers on his head."

I tried to console Tucky and said, "Thar, thar," and I patted her on the back.

"Ain't nothin or nobody around here but us," I went on.

"He held back a hatchet at me," Tucky said. "He say, 'Ain't no nigger kin kill me withouten I kill her.' He drawed back. He were bloody."

"Well, he didn't kill you, now did he? All it were was a dream. And I don't take no stock in dreams except they can scare the daylights out of you. The best way to look at it is this: ain't it a good feelin when you wake up and everthing is all right?"

Tucky told me to hush. "I heared noise off yondah."

I listened and didn't hear nothing.

"Hit were a haint. I heared it on the leaves."

"It were not no haint. They isn't such a thing. Like I told you, Hiwasse is kin to all them dead Indians and so am I. So are you, because you're colored. They'd be scared to death of Hiwasse because of the way he likes to fight so much. Now you settle down, Tucky, and don't work yourself into a spell."

Hiwasse had started mumbling and rolling around. Finally he set up.

"What're you up to? I thought everbody had went to sleep."

"We had," I told him, "but Tucky was havin a bad dream and she has got it in her head that she hears the haints of them dead Indians in the mounds. I told her them Indians wouldn't bother none of us, especially with you here."

"Hell, nah," Hiwasse said. "They all like me and any of my friends. Tucky, this here is the best place on earth you could be. That is, if you wanted to be pertected. If I'm ever on the run, right here is whur I come to. Right here is whur I feel at ease."

He asked Tucky if she didn't want a little whisky to settle her mind, but I told him before Tucky could answer him that maybe she wasn't old enough yet.

"I give it to my own younguns," Hiwasse said. "It settles them down."

Hiwasse told Tucky to ease herself and he'd sing her a song that he use to do in the rodeo. He'd come out riding on a hoss and wearing feathers and at about the middle of the arena he'd get off of his hoss and step up to the microphone:

I'm ridin my hoss
To the end of the road.

I'm reapin the crop
From the evil I've sowed.
Oh huntin ground, oh huntin ground,
Oh happy happy huntin ground.

The white folks come
And took my land.
I took their scalps
With my bloody hand.
Oh huntin ground, oh huntin ground,
I want you happy huntin ground.
I'll smoke my peace pipe
Day and night,
Won't ever have
To get a light,
Just watch the maidens
Come and go
Without strong wind
Or rain or snow.
Oh huntin ground, oh huntin ground,
Oh happy happy huntin ground.

Hiwasse went on to say that when he got finished he'd get back on the horse, bow his head down, and ride slow out of the arena. The band would have some drums rolling like thunder.

When Hiwasse had got to the part in his song about the scalps and the bloody hand, I was afraid it might do something bad to Tucky. It didn't seem to, because when Hiwasse had got through with all he had to sing and say, Tucky had went off to sleep.

As far as I know she didn't wake up again till it was day. I didn't, and I don't think Hiwasse did.

Chapter 12

IT MUST OF BEEN a right smart up in the morning when I commenced to open my eyes. It was already hot. First thing I noticed when I got my eyes to where they would work was what looked like a bunch of big flattened-out anthills with grass growing on them. Then it come to my head that them was the Indian mounds. They was a sight of them, and they went back and back, and I don't know how far they went. I thought, I wonder who buried the last ones that didn't have nobody to bury them. I decided I'd forget about that or maybe ask Hiwasse later.

Hiwasse was about twenty-thirty foot away and had a little fire going. He'd sharpened a stick and stuck it into some pork that he was heating over the fire.

When he seen I was awake he said, "Fixin some breakfast. This here hot pork is good. Come and fix some."

I tried to limber up my back a little. Tucky was still asleep and I thought I'd let her rest till I was sure I'd got myself awake. That's one thing I never could do was come right awake. When ma and pa woke up they'd act like they never had been asleep and their minds would be active and alert. Me, I'd always have to think where I was and what day it was, and then when I'd got to studying it, it would seem like it was all too much for me and I'd just want to go back to sleep and forget the whole thing.

That's the way I felt right then. I didn't even want the day before to be a memory. And I sure wasn't ready for no plans for my day's journey of this day.

I kind of shambled over to where Hiwasse was and of course Hiwasse turned out to be one of them folks like ma and pa that wakes up clear of head and making big plans for everything in sight and out of sight.

Hiwasse had taken him a mouth of pork meat and was talking away. "This here's the way I figure it," he said, "they gonna search Bennett high and low for me and when they see I ain't to be found they're gonna strike out on the road—"

"Who?" I said. "Who air you talking about? What road?"

He give me a look like I was addle-minded. "Who do you think?"

"I can't think. I'm half asleep and my body's stiff."

"The ιιιυν. Willie Joe Crawford and his buddies. And the policemen, if the ιιιυν could convince them that Hiwasse has done some bad unholy deeds. They're liable to be out on the road to Manfred City, lookin for both you and me. Now, that's who and that's what. Here, heat up some pork."

He handed me the stick and a hunk of meat, and I held it over the fire.

Somebody from behind me said, "Mawnin, mawnin. It be hot awready." That was Tucky. And that reminded me I had to go relieve myself, and if I said I was going anywhere on earth Tucky would probably be right at my heels.

"Mawnin, Tucky," I said and Hiwasse said the same thing.

"Did you sleep good?" I wanted to know. "And did you have any more bad dreams?"

"Nawsuh. Mr. Hiwasse taken keer of the haints."

Hiwasse grunted and smiled at that, taking full credit for all control of the haints. He got to telling Tucky how Indian haints wouldn't ever come back to scare good folks, only the bad ones. Even though he was making the haints out to be awful nice, he was still breaking down everything that I'd tried to put in Tucky's head. But Tucky seemed to like it better the way Hiwasse was explaining it than the way I had did it.

"I'll be back in a few minutes," I said. "I got to be about my private business."

I got off as quick as I could, while Hiwasse was still on his story, and Tucky didn't have a chance to come trailing behind me.

We set around for a while that morning, not making no effort to rush ourselves. Hiwasse had several drinks of whisky and I had three-four. Tucky played the radio. I searched around and found me a spring where Bessie

163

could drink. Everything was good and lazy, with Hiwasse telling about his adventures and fights and some of the women he had knowed. I could of set there forever just listening, with no thoughts at all about going on with my journey to Manfred City.

Hiwasse told about when he acted as a clean-up boy at a gambling house in New Orleans. He said he wasn't as old as me by a long shot. He'd sweep the floors, help throw out customers that got drunk or mad or both, service one of the gals that worked there by the name of Teena. It was Teena that had got him some broke ribs and lost him his job. Two-three times a week him and Teena would go off to her place and have their pleasure there. They wasn't but one bad drawback, Hiwasse said, and that was his boss, a Mr. Fauchet, who had took it in mind that all of the gals that worked for him was for his own particular pleasure and nobody else's. Especially, Hiwasse said, not no young bastard of Cherokee blood that was hired for clean-up. So one day Hiwasse and Teena was laying around on silky sheets, guzzling the whisky, and having a general good time, when all of a sudden in comes Mr. Fauchet breaking the door down along with two big niggers. (Tucky told him they was colored people, and Hiwasse said he was sorry and that it was two big colored men that come in.) All Mr. Fauchet said was, "Make him feel worse, boys," and they did. They knocked him all over the room so's he ended up with some broke ribs and his face so swole up he couldn't see out of it.

"Whut happen to Teena?" Tucky wanted to know. Tucky was stretched back against a pine tree like she was the Queen of Sheba and having the time of her life.

164

"Ah," Hiwasse said, "she got fired. But she got worse'n that. Mr. Fauchet had them two niggers—colored folks —cut up her face with a razor so she wouldn't be beautiful no more and so she couldn't get a job at nothin no better'n puttin on exhibitions. He took Teena to his gamblin house and showed her off to the other gals, so's they'd know what would happen to them if they was to get out of line."

Hiwasse was looking off to where the Indian mounds was and way beyond them. It seemed like he was talking more to all of them dead Indians than he was talking to us.

"Mr. Fauchet he give me twenty dollars and told me to go off from New Orleans. He said to not ever try to take advantage of your boss that has been good to you. He said he might of made me rich someday." Hiwasse stopped and throwed a pine cone at the fire. "Well, I'm as rich as you see me right now."

"We ain't gonna get no richer settin here all day," I said and don't know why I said it because I was purely content to stay right there and not be no richer or poorer. It was one of them things you say because it seems like you ought to.

"Less be up and at it," Hiwasse said. "Up and at it, Tucky."

"Yassuh."

We went to the edge of the woods so's we could look out over the road for any signs of the IIIUN. Both left and right it looked clear and peaceful as could be— nothing but a long strip of gravel road to the left in the direction of Bennett, and a short strip of road down to a curve in the direction of Manfred City.

"Whyn't we try to make it on the road fer a while?"
I said. "Shorely them ɪɪɪᴜɴᴇrs ain't gonna be out
lookin fer us this time of day. Shorely they got more to
do than be bloodhoundin us."

Tucky looked up at Hiwasse and said, "Shorely."

"Bloodhoundin us is their prime concern," he said.
"But I'd as soon try the road. I don't wanta bust up this
here motor scooter. It took a lot of my brain to get this
here machine."

"You'd be better off with a hoss," I said. "A hoss
can live on willpower. That's somethin you can't say of
a machine."

"Nah. Less go. I'll ride down to that bend and wait
for you and your hoss's willpower till it gets you there.
A helluva way to get to Manfred City." Hiwasse give a
big roaring laugh, and off he went.

"Tucky, what would you druther ride on, a scooter or
a hoss?" I said.

Tucky waited a little before answering. She was either
studying about it or she liked the scooter best and
wanted to tell me polite so's my feelings wouldn't be
hurt.

"Hoss," she said, "if I ain't in no herry."

Hiwasse had zipped away before you could think
about it and was past the bend. Tucky and I took our
time, talking about this and that, till we got down to
the bend and around it. There wasn't any Hiwasse.

"Tuck," I said, "where is that Cherokee at?"

"Hit beat me." Then she said, "Theah his tracks."

There they were, across a low ditch and then over
red dirt to where there was the beginning of woods.

I said, "What you reckin he's went off in there fer?

Ain't he had enough of woods to last him a little while? After last night?"

"Indians wants woods," Tucky said.

"Well, we'll go see what he's about."

I decided to tie Bessie just inside the thicket because the trees and bushes was close together and the branches was low. Me and Tucky followed where the growth had been broke down by the motor scooter. It seemed like we was going a awful long ways. All of a sudden Tucky jerked at my overalls and said, "Be still."

I could hear voices and a lots of them. I whispered to Tucky for us to move up quiet as we could. I didn't have no notion of what we was heading for. I knowed one thing from the last two-three days, and that was to enter careful, it don't matter what.

We eased on and on till the trees got scarcer and then smack in your face was blue sky straight ahead of you. The land we was walking on took a sudden dip and went straight into a kind of valley below us. Down there where we had a good view of it all, they was what looked like a arena and it was full of people in hoods and sheets and other things to cover them up, all setting or squatting in a kind of audience. Up in front of them was a cross made out of boards and tied to it was Hiwasse stripped down to the waist. On one side of him, and I nearly dropped dead, was the Lord Jesus Turner in his civilian clothes. On the other side and not wearing a hood was Willie Joe Crawford. Even from a distance his face looked mighty beat-up and swole.

Tucky had hold of my overalls and was about to pull one of the galluses off of my shoulder.

167

"Is they gwine to crucify Hiwasse?" she said.

"Don't know. Less try to listen and hear whut they say."

It looked like Willie Joe Crawford was about primed to give some kind of a speech because he had his arms spread-eagle and was waving his fingers for the rest of the IIIUNers to get quiet.

"Y'all know," he started off with what seemed to me like a high-pitched voice for such a man in power, "what this here—I started to say man but I won't say man—what this here animal, whose blood ain't the same as my blood and yore blood, whose fambly was savages and has left him to us a savage too, whose ancestrals cut off the very scalps of yore ancestrals and left them to bleed and die and raped their beloved women—"

I wanted to know what on earth he was ever going to get at.

"—y'all know that he don't worship the same God as y'all worship who is repasented here before you as the Lord Jesus Christ Turner, Father, Son, and Holy Ghost . . ." Willie Joe stopped to get his breath. "Y'all know what he has did at this perticler time, which was by way of tryin to defame a white woman of American rights and heritage, and who could of been yore wife are mother are daughter but who was my wife of holy matrimony and loved in my home by me and my eight-month-old baby boy—"

The Lord Jesus Turner hollered out, "Amen! Name of me!"

"Y'all know whut my wife has told me this vary mornin, that this savage—and scum from the swamp deeps—perposed to my wife last night, in the filthiest

168

of whorehouse language, that she perticipate with him in sex relations that was not only unholy but was unnatural to boot."

He stopped again to get his breath, and he started to wipe his face with a rag but must of thought about it being so raw, because he put the rag back in his pocket.

"That ain't so," I told Tucky. "Hiwasse didn't say nothin like that to Willie Joe Crawford's wife. It was his wife that was flirtin with Hiwasse and me both. He ain't tellin nothin but lies."

"Who gonna know that?" Tucky said.

"What I perpose," Willie Joe went on, "is to cut out that part of this savage's body that was the cause of him tawkin any sech way as he done to my wife!"

All of the mUNers let out a big holler.

"Thataway, he can't leave planted nowhur no future savages to prey on yore daughters and their daughters and maybe even yore wives and mothers too.

"I perpose futher that when we have operated on him to the good of the people and in the name of the Lord, that we leave him here to lay, stropped to the cross, symbolical of the sacrifice that ever has to be made fer the decent folks and fer the future of their blood and their younguns.

"We will not have rape and murder and unnatural acts performed on our white ladies by the Indians, the niggers, the Catholics, the Jews, the Commonists, the heatherns of any type, shape, color, religion, or country!"

I thought to myself that Willie Joe Crawford had just about covered everbody on earth including hisself.

I said, "Tucky, he's got it in fer us."

169

"If y'all agree with what I perpose, let me hear you holler loud!"

Not only did they holler but they acted like they had went crazy, jumping up and down, squealing, whistling, running here and yonder. You'd of thought gold was struck or that they all was the daddy of their first youngun.

I said to Tucky, "We might could overlook them fer bein crazy people, but they're gonna do somethin bad to Hiwasse." I didn't know if Tucky understood what they was planning to do. I think she did.

Willie Joe finally got all of them quiet and settled down and said, "I'm gonna call on the Lord Jesus Turner to speak to us now, to give us a blessin, and to guide us in general."

The Lord Jesus said, "Amen. Amen. This here infidel stropped to the cross on which I once was stropped myself and who I can tell by the look in his eye and by the way his hair stands that he ain't saved, don't need to be breedin much less suckin up the good air on this earth which is mine and—"

The Lord Jesus went on and on with his regular kind of talk but it didn't seem to me he was as forceful as when I'd talked to him and when he'd stood before Oli-Oli's converted savages. They was something wrong with him.

While he was talking Willie Joe Crawford was flashing around a big hunting knife, part of the time at the crowd and part of the time right in Hiwasse's face. After while he stuck the knife in the ground and then ripped open Hiwasse's pants and undershorts to where he was going to be cut out.

170

I said, "Tucky, don't look."

"I's gwine to," she said.

"Well, Hiwasse wouldn't like it if he knowed about it."

"Hit ain't nothin I ain't seed."

The Lord Jesus Turner was still going on and had got the Virgin Mary into it, along with his Dreama Glory.

Right then it come to my head: you have got the nail in yore pocket. You have got his strength. He ain't doin nothin but mouthin up words and he knows it. You have got him in yore power and have got all of them InjUN-ers too, as shore as yore name is Rover Youngblood.

I made up my mind to go down there with the nail and do the best I could with it.

I told Tucky, "I am goin to go and perform a miracle with a nail."

"Whut?"

"You watch me. I have now became the Lord Jesus Youngblood. You set right here and don't move except if I fail in my miracle. If I was to fail, you head out fer Bessie and hide till all this bunch is gone. Ain't nothin they'd enjoy more'n gettin a hold of a colored youngun."

I started down the hill, stumbling some but making it as quick as I could. I was gonna have to give a speech before Willie Joe Crawford give his first lick with that knife.

"Mr. Turner!" I hollered. *"Mr. Turner!"*

They all started to turn around to look at me. Finally the Lord Jesus seen them turning and he turned too. He couldn't hear me above his own racket.

"Mr. Turner! You ain't the Lord Jesus Christ or the

171

Father or the Son or Holy Ghost no more'n that savage Indian is who you are about to persecute."

Now I was at the bottom of the hill at the edge of the arena, not far from the audience, making my way toward them up front.

"You know dad-blame well that it's me that is the Lord Jesus by name of Youngblood, name of Father, Son, and Holy Ghost, that is me. I got here in my hand, and I hold it up fer one and all to look at, the nail from the crucifixtion that is symbolical of the Lord Jesus Christ and that gives him his strength and his power of salvation. Name of me."

I was holding the nail way up over my head, and right now I was not more than ten foot from Lord Jesus. He wasn't saying a word but standing with his mouth open and looked like he was scared to death. Willie Joe Crawford and all the IIIUNers didn't as much as move or let out a sound.

All that I was saying was way loud and in a strained voice.

I looked direct at Lord Jesus. *"You know you have backslid. I can tell by yore eyes and by the way yore hair is standin and by the way yore feet is planted on the ground that you ain't saved, much less the Lord Jesus Christ.*

"I perdict that if you don't do like I say and kneel down right now this minute to me, that a bolt of lightning will strike you from the sky and that you will find yore soul as well as yore body the next second in hell, both burnin and sizzlin and poppin eternally. Kneel!"

I don't know what I would of did if he hadn't of

172

kneeled. He kneeled. To add to it all, especially for the rest of them people, I run over to Lord Jesus and swiped the nail across his face, causing it to bleed.

The whole crowd let out a kind of "ah" sound. The Lord Jesus started taking on like I'd about killed him and fell face down in the dirt. I thought to myself about the last time he'd been face down in the dirt. He started bawling like a baby and saying, "Don't. Don't."

I said, *"If you don't stop that bawlin I'm gonna turn loose this here savage and have him cut on you and Willie Joe Crawford and everbody else, like you was gonna cut on him. In the name of me!"*

Till now I hadn't give Hiwasse any kind of notice with my eyes because I didn't want to take my mind off of what I was doing. I give him a quick look and he seemed to think I had either went crazy or that I was what I said I was, the Lord Jesus Christ Youngblood. One would of been about as bad as the other as far as Hiwasse was concerned.

I said to Willie Joe Crawford, *"I want you to let aloose that there savage Cherokee Indian. When you have got that did, I'll tell you more."*

Willie Joe started to doing it like he was in his sleep. I had to keep talking so's that nobody there would have time to think for hisself and wouldn't have but one notion, which was that I might strike them dead or bring fire, famine, and general hell to them.

"You folks ain't as good as the spit out of the devil's mouth, settin out yonder on the mornin grass, actin like a bunch of younguns when you oughta be at home praisin me. Oh, it'll take a long time afore I forgive ye fer this."

I seen that Hiwasse was set free and had pulled his pants back together.

I said to him, *"Go unto the hills with the blessin I perclaim to ye now,"* and I pointed up to where Tucky was hiding, *"and turn from yore savage ways because I see that yore hair is beginnin to stand right. Go!"*

Hiwasse grabbed his shirt and struck out.

"You!" I pointed to Willie Joe Crawford. *"Kneel!"*

He done it. I held the nail out in front of me like it was a snake and guiding me toward him.

"This here nail has got the power to bring the dead back to life. It has also got the power to bring death to the living. What is it you want? Don't tell me, because you ain't got the right to say."

One of the few places on his head that wasn't beat-up was his forehead. I swiped across it with the nail. He didn't take on as bad as the Lord Jesus did.

"That there sign that I have struck on yore flesh can mean one of two things, that you might live or die. Whichaway it is lays to yore thinkin. As long as I don't step in myself.

"These here is my final words before I go to the fields and the hills and the countryside in general: cast off them mortal rags which is sheets and hoods and other manners of sinful dress. Now! I mean now!"

They all started to take off their mortal rags. Most of them had on their regular clothes underneath but some had on just their underwear. Willie Joe looked like he had on the same undershirt that he was wearing at the Top Hat the night before. For sure, he still had them same tattoos.

"When I leave this here valley and make my ascen-

174

sion, I want each and ever one to set here for one hour and not say nothin to nobody else. Then I want each and ever one of you to go back to yore own house and tell yore kinfolks what a sin you've been livin in. I want you to hear and now make a promise to yoreself to strike out agin the IIIUN—*because it ain't you, it's me. And I'd as soon to strike you dead, put a curse on yore kin, dry up yore milk cows, burn down yore houses, and anythin else that was to come to my mind."*

I was getting ready to run for the hill.

"Look at this here nail." I waited for just a little so's they could all take it in. *"Bow yore heads, shet yore eyes, and stay that way till thunder comes in yore minds. Now!"*

They did and I got up that hill as fast as I could.

Whur, I thought, is Hiwasse's motor scooter?

Chapter 13

HIWASSE'S MOTOR SCOOTER, it turned out, was throwed back in some brush near the road.

As soon I'd got up that hill me and Hiwasse and Tucky struck for the road as fast as we could.

Hiwasse kept wanting to know what was all of this business about the nail. Tucky thought I was magic and didn't want to get on Bessie with me. I told both of them that I'd explain everything to them later on but right now we ought to get away as fast as we could. No telling what might happen. Them IIIUNers might not care if a curse was put on their kin or not. And they might not care if their milk cows went dry.

I said to Bessie, "Honey, you goin to have to make tracks. This here is one of them times when we can't have no regards fer personal feelins and discomforts.

If we don't make haste, you may not have nobody to feed and water you."

Hiwasse's scooter was going prrrattt-prrrattt, and he said he'd go down the road aways till he found a shade tree and wait for us.

"Don't be took in by no strangers," I told him, "whuther they be man of God or man of the devil."

He touched hisself at the crotch and said, "I fer one ain't talkin to no-body." Then he laughed and tore down the road.

I said to Tucky, "Hold on tight. Don't drop the radio." Then to Bessie, "Giddap!"

Off we went sailing, Bessie stretching her legs like she hadn't stretched them in a long time. It give me a fine feeling to have the good air striking me in the face and to think maybe that I'd got rid of the IIIUN and the Lord Jesus Turner for good.

Several things was on my mind, and a good many questions. The questions went something like this:

1. Where was the Virgin Mary? Why hadn't she been with the Lord Jesus Turner at the IIIUN meeting? Would the IIIUN not allow no women?

2. Was that nail I had in my pocket as important to the strength of the Lord Jesus Turner as it seemed to be? Was them IIIUNers just dumbfounded by me waving that nail around or had that nail give me some kind of special power? Was the nail magic just for the Lord Jesus Turner and not for me? Because I didn't feel no different except scared to death because of what might of happened to me a little while back.

3. Would all of them that the Lord Jesus Turner had

blessed come unblessed now? Such as Oli-Oli and his converted savages, not to mention the folks all over the country that the Lord Jesus had took a hand with.

4. Would the Virgin Mary turn back into a civilian by name of Ava Maureen and maybe go back into show business?

5. What was the difference between the Lord Jesus who was Turner and now was maybe Youngblood and the Lord Jesus that was the one my ma believed in?

6. Would the whole country be tore up by all the change that had been made?

7. What on earth would my ma and pa say if somebody was to tell them their son was the Lord Jesus Youngblood and they was Joseph and Mary?

8. What would Miss Mary Dove Truman think?

Here went my answers, the best I could figure them out:

1. They wasn't no telling where the Virgin Mary might be. She might be drunk on homebrew. She might of got beat up by the Lord Jesus because she give me this nail. Like as not if she'd of been well and happy, she'd of been at the IIIUN meeting whether they allowed women or not.

2. I couldn't understand nothing about that nail. It evidently done something special to the Lord Jesus Turner. I was happy it had saved mine and Hiwasse's life but like I said I didn't find myself changed a whole lot inside of me.

3. If Oli-Oli and all of them that had been saved and converted was to come unsaved, there might be general destruction. On the other hand things might get better. We'd have to wait and see.

178

4. I had a strong feeling that the Virgin Mary would be awful happy to return to being a civilian and take up with show business again. By nature she seemed to take more to the body than she did to the spirit, and she shore loved to put on a party dress. Now her homebrew wouldn't be sanctified but she'd probably not drink no more than when it was sanctified. She might drink less, because she wouldn't have to take it for holy occasions.

5. I didn't have no answer to this. Somebody like my ma or Miss Mary Dove would have to figure it out.

6. This shift could be something like the crucifixtion but not the same thing a bit—mainly a shift of power.

7. My ma and pa would drop dead if they was to think they was Joseph and Mary. Especially my pa. He'd drop dead twice by being told that I was the Lord Jesus. He wouldn't get to whup me.

8. Wasn't no telling what Miss Mary Dove would think. I wanted to know.

While I'd been doing all this thinking, Tucky had been playing the radio as loud as she could get it. I didn't pay it no mind till now that I'd got the questions and answers out of my head. The Opelika Sundogs was coming on with Western-style religious music. They was singing something about going to Jesus in a covered wagon. I thought to myself, What if they was to think it was me they was talking about? Me on a hoss and them in a covered wagon.

I said to Tucky, "Shet that down a little bit, please, ma'am. It's too much racket after whut I've went through this mornin."

She did and said, "Scuse me."

179

After a little she said, "You gwine fergive me?"

"To whut?"

"Fergive me."

"Fer whut? What air you tawkin about?"

"Fer that man I kilt."

"You saved my life," I said. "Ain't no call fer me to fergive you."

"Now you be Jesus."

"Aw. Don't think about it. Act like I'm Rover."

We had came to a shade tree, a big oak, with Hiwasse stretched out under it spread-eagled and didn't look like he had a care in the world. I thought to myself, If it warn't fer the nail in my pocket he'd be stretched out on the cross with his manhood cut out and bleedin to death and like as not the wild animals chewin him to pieces.

"Howdy," I hollered.

He'd been dozing off and jumped right up. He might of thought it was some of the IIIUN after him.

"Howdy," he said. "You got here quicker'n I thought you would. You must of put a motor in that hoss."

"Naw," I said. "Bessie goes by free will."

I let Bessie rest for a few minutes because she'd got so hot she was lathering against my legs. Tucky wanted to be excused and me and Hiwasse promised we'd look the other way. She taken the radio with her and had it playing.

Hiwasse said, "It ain't far now to Manfred City. Ain't no use in me waitin on you till we get to the outskirts. I tell you what"—and he studied a piece of grass that he'd pulled up—"they's a big filling station about a mile out, white-painted concrete, Texaco, with a big star, and is owned by a man named of Urig Genter. I'll wait

180

for you there and put my motor scooter in back. Awright?"

Tucky had came back and I told her to cut down the radio some.

"Now when you're thar take the hoss around back and hitch her up. I'll be waitin inside fer you."

"Do I have to give any special signals?"

"Nah. I'll be settin, like as not, tawkin to Urig." He taken a thumb and hit it against his chest. "I got connections, boy."

"You didn't have enough to save yoreself from nearly bein cut on by Willie Joe Crawford," I told him. "Seems like it was me that had the connections. Seems like it was me that performed a miracle."

"Hit were," Tucky said.

Hiwasse let out a laugh and said, "It was somethin and I don't know rightly what it was but it wasn't no miracle."

I looked down the road from where we'd come.

"One thing is shore," I said, "we better make tracks. I ain't aimin to cause two miracles in the same day, one right after another."

Me and Hiwasse decided that maybe it would be better if Tucky was to ride with him because, like I put it,

"She warn't in on the miracle and besides, it's one thing fer a Cherokee to excape from the IIIUN but it's somethin else for a colored gal to do it."

Tucky didn't want to go with Hiwasse because she said I had all the power in my pocket and she'd got use to it. I had the notion that the main reason she wanted to stay with me was because she thought I might take the radio away from her.

"You hang on to that air radio, Tucky," I said, "because I might drop it."

She seemed to pert up to that, and then they left, making more dust and racket than it seemed like they needed to.

I said, "Bessie, here we go one more time and hit looks like we's gettin close to the end. Seems like we got a right to have us some rest."

I started to think about Manfred City and that right soon it would be all around me. It would be like having a new moon with clear sky when everthing is different and you see the hills and hollers and sometimes a wild animal scampering along, or you see the branch of a pine tree that you never have saw before.

I could remember times like that when me and my brothers would go out to look by a new moon and it would seem like I was in a different world from the one there at Clearpoint.

I knowed I'd have to get use to things like the Lord Jesus Turner's car that didn't make little or no sense to me and I'd have to get use to songs like them that Ursula liked so much and said was fabulous, and to show business like Virgin Mary Turner or Ava Maureen, whichever, had once been in.

But here was the way I looked at it: they was some good things that I already knowed about, like that kind of whisky that Ursula and me had dranken which you had to compare with the kind that Lord Jesus Turner blessed for Oli-Oli and his converted savages and others, and they was things like Miss Mary Dove Truman's radio that run on batteries and didn't have to be plugged in.

I wondered to myself, Do they allow the miuners and sech? Will they put up with the likes of Willie Joe Crawford and that man with long hair that wanted to charge me and Tucky for going across the county and that made Tucky kill him?

I reckined we wouldn't be freed of all of that. And I couldn't see myself so much the Lord Jesus Youngblood already that I could put a stop to all of it at once.

What if it was truly so that that nail in my pocket was what it was suppose to be?

I could stop the wars and rumors of wars but then Miss Mary Dove might not have enough to listen to on the radio.

I could build Mr. Joe Two a picture show right by his house and put a bed in it so's he could look at Shirley Temple and Will Rogers all the time, and if it was to be a sin him doing it, then I could forgive him for it. But Miss Mary Dove might get lonesome for his racket and wish he was back in bed in his own room. I didn't think she'd want to stay there in the picture show with him all the time.

I could make pa so's he never would want to whup me again and would smile more and let ma and the younguns think he taken more of a interest in them.

I could get ma all the laying hens she wanted.

I could get party dresses for Lamour Anne and Naomi.

I could do this and I could do that. I went on in my head, seeing what would be good and then what would be bad about it.

I commenced to think of a aunt on my ma's side by name of Aunt Billie who was fat as a sow hog full of its litter and was always sweating and had lots of powder on her face and neck. They would be rings around her neck at the wrinkles where the powder had sweated off.

Ma always said for us not to call her fat but to think of her as having a overweight problem and for each one of us younguns to remember we like as not had some problems of our own, and how would we like for folks to make fun of them?

It seemed like Aunt Billie had more problems than anybody else because for one thing she was a old maid even if she was always going on about how Hutch Woodard or Sam Rainey was trying to get her to marry them and that she wouldn't have nothing to do with such stuff as that, because Hutch dranken too heavy and Sam didn't make enough money and so forth.

Aunt Billie herself didn't have no money, not even to speak of, and the whole family had to chip in ever month as shore as the sun and moon to keep her in fancy clothes and a little house and buy her face powder and the likes.

Of course since she was a old maid she didn't have no younguns that would be a comfort to her in her olden days. She let on that she didn't care for younguns a bit, and when me and my brothers and sisters was little and we'd be playing or making some kind of a racket we'd have to hush up or play Be Quiet or go off from the house somewheres.

About once a week she'd bring her sewing or knitting or crocheting and set with ma on the front porch and rock.

She'd say to ma things like these here:

"If it's one thing I don't like, it's the way yore old

man makes a slave out of you. You coulda married better if you'd awaited."

"Them younguns you give life to, they is outa control, outa control. They'll ever one end up in the pens and whorehouses. But they're better'n some. That ain't sayin much."

"It seems like to me that a womern that's too skinny is tacky. It don't show no vitality in her. Looks like she don't respect what God's give her and sticks up her nose at His bounty."

"Folks that grubs after money is grubbin after the devil because when you grub down deep enough in the dirt you'll shore strike hell and that's whur you gonna find the devil. Seems to me like everbody oughta be pore but well-off and respected."

After Aunt Billie would of left and maybe pa would of heared some of this, he'd let off with a bunch of hell-fires and damnations.

"Who in thunder does that fat sow think she is?" he'd let out.

Ma would like as not mumble something that nobody couldn't hear.

"Wouldn't no man in Alabama waste a eye-blink on her, if he warn't blind."

Ma would be setting some biscuits before him.

"The face powder on her face comes outa my pocket not to mention the trash clothes kiverin up her fat ass!"

Ma'd say, "Pa."

"She wants younguns to keep quiet, let her go out and brood some with a blindman! The first un she can find that ain't got no feelin to his body!"

Pa would sum it all up by shoving his chair back

from the table and saying, "What Miss Billie wants is fer everbody to be like she is and fer her to be like whatever she wants to be! What she wants to be is God-amighty Hisself! Hit's the truth!"

Chapter 14

I HADN'T BEEN PAYING no mind much to the country around me, just riding along and studying in my head about Aunt Billie, when I commenced to take notice and from what I seen over to my right I knowed I was coming to somewheres but it looked to me like it were more to somewheres bad than to somewheres good.

Starting right up close to the road and then going down into a dip and then up a hill and way off into yonder, they was ever piece, shape, kind, or form of automobile that was probably knowed to man. They was fenders, tops, wheels, general-looking pieces, motors that was ever color you could think of including rusted. Lots of them automobiles was whole but busted-up and it was a curiosity to me why anybody in his right mind would want to keep all of that junk.

Ma had a collection of buttons that was odds and ends

that she couldn't use on nothing but that she didn't want to throw out because some of them buttons was purty to look at. Brother Silas had a bug collection that even me myself could take some interest in and besides that his teacher said it was educational. I could go on with what each one in my family collected, and whatever it was made some kind of sense to me, but this here man who had collected all of these pieces of automobiles didn't make no sense to me a bit.

One thing was it looked to me like he'd got hisself too big a collection and another thing was it looked hainted, like all of them pieces might start coming at you or like all of them might gather up together into one and start coming.

"Bessie, don't look," I said. "Keep goin as fast as you can go. We got some kind of a haint or a crazy man around us and Rover Youngblood or Lord Jesus Youngblood, either one, I don't want no part of it. Giddap! Giddap!"

The sun itself didn't seem to care none for all of that mess because they wasn't much sparkle that come off of it and what they was was ugly-looking. It seemed like we went by it for a mile but I knowed it couldn't be a mile because it wasn't but a mile in all to where we was going.

When I spotted the big white Texaco station and seen the star I felt lots better, even if that mess did go right up to the side of it.

Out in front they was a man putting gasoline in a car but I didn't stop to say howdy or nothing but went whizzing around to the back of the station where I was proud to see Hiwasse's scooter.

I tied Bessie to a pipe and said, "Bessie, we got through that. We might could get through anything. You cool off fer a little."

Around in front the man was still standing with his hose to the car. I couldn't decide how old he looked to be. He had a beard that was gray and black and come nearly down to his waist and he was wearing brown-looking pants and shirt with grease on them.

I went up and said, "Howdy. I am looking fer a man name of Mr. Urig Genter. My name is Rover Young-blood." I didn't think I'd better use the Lord Jesus on him.

He had thick eyebrows that hung down some over his eyes.

He said, "I was named Urig Genter by the woman that through her labor brought me into the world. I am still named it." He waited a minute and said, "What's in a name?"

I told him I didn't know. I noticed that his way of talking was not a bit like that at Clearpoint.

He asked me again, "What's in a name?"

I said, "Well," and that's as far as I got.

He shut off the gas and told me, "Hiwasse and that nigger child is setting in yonder in the back room. You go through the front room and there's a door that says PRIVATE. You go through that door and there you'll find Hiwasse and that nigger child."

I thanked him and went into the station to the door that said PRIVATE. I knocked on it.

"Who is it?" come a voice I knowed to be Hiwasse's.

"It's Rover."

"Come on."

He was setting in a rocker holding to a bottle of whisky and Tucky was on a straight chair looking at a magazine and listening to the radio. They looked as peaceful as could be and like they might of been setting there all of their lives.

"Shorely that hoss didn't get you here," Hiwasse said and had a big grin on his face.

"I got here," I said, "and it warn't by no motor scooter that could of played out on me."

Tucky come up and taken my hand for just a minute and then went back to her chair.

"Have a snort of this here," Hiwasse said and handed me the bottle.

I taken a big snort and it was good, like that Ursula had gave me.

"That's shore fine," I said.

Hiwasse told me, "Set down over there and rest up. We can start to take it easy."

I set down and studied the room some. They wasn't much to it to speak of—white walls, four-five chairs, a shelf full of books, four-five empty whisky bottles, two-three full ones, a old stove, some greasy rags, some pictures of neckid women on the wall that I hoped Tucky wouldn't notice.

"Whut was all of that thar?" I said to Hiwasse. "On the side of the road. All of them parts of cars. I ain't never saw sech."

"That was a car graveyard," he said, "whur they put the dead."

I wanted to know why they didn't cover them up like they did other dead things and he said he didn't know.

When I said it looked hainted, Tucky give me a look.

190

I told her, "I don't mean the kind of haints you mean, Tucky," and that seemed to relieve her. She got back to her magazine.

"I wanta know about that there nail," Hiwasse said, "that and yore miracle."

I told him the whole story about the nail and Lord Jesus Turner, Ava Maureen or whatever, and all of it.

Hiwasse had been grinning while I told my story and when I got through with it he slapped his leg and let out a holler.

"I wouldn't be so shore," I said, "that they ain't nothin to this here nail." I taken it out of my pocket to let him see it.

"Hand it here," he told me.

"Naw," I said, "I can't do that."

"That nail is a old nail that's got rust on it and that's all there is to it," he said.

"Hit's magic," Tucky said.

Hiwasse got ready to say a ugly word and thought better of it. "It's a nail," he ended up.

"You might live to see differnt," I said. "Hit saved yore life."

All Hiwasse done was take a long swaller of whisky and rock in his rocker like he owned the earth.

"That nail makes me come to think of the voodoo charms that a old nigger woman in New—"

"Colored," Tucky said.

"Awright, colored. She had two dried-up fingers of a baby that died when it was a day old. This here old voodoo woman claimed she could rub them fingers on somebody's picture that you brought her and make whoever it was die or do whatever you wanted."

191

He studied his whisky bottle and didn't have no grin on his face. "They might of been somethin to it because I was told by good sources that it was the truth, but I ain't sayin it was the truth. Anyhow"—and he was grinning again—"that don't mean that old rusty nail you got can do nothin. Haw."

If Tucky hadn't of been there I might of told him what to do and where to go. Instead I said, "Gimme another drink of that good whisky," which he done.

"Hiwasse," I told him, "here we are right outside of Manfred City which I ain't never saw or saw nothin like and we got to make plans. One thing is what about"— and I nodded my head toward Tucky and said instead— "gettin a job."

He knowed what I meant and knowed like I did that I couldn't go on looking after a young child that was a nigger to boot. It grieved me that I couldn't because I liked Tucky besides the fact that she'd saved my life.

"I'll figger out for us," Hiwasse said.

He finished off that bottle of whisky and started off on another one. I wondered how much whisky a full-blooded Cherokee could drink on a more or less empty stomach without falling flat on his face or going crazy. We'd studied at school in Clearpoint how the Indians would go crazy on drink.

A picture come to my mind of Hiwasse stripped down to the waist and war paint all over him, running around the room with a tommyhawk, and me going in one direction and Tucky in the other with her radio playing gospel music.

"I done got things figgered out," I said.

192

"How's that?" he asked me and looked like he didn't believe me.

"I got a place here in Manfred City whur I can go to find out about a job or whatever I need. And that goes fer you too, I'm shore."

"Whur's it at?"

Just then Urig come busting in and set down in one of the straight chairs.

"Clint's took over for the night shift," he said. "Hand me the whisky, Hiwasse."

There in the room it seemed like Urig had more hair on him than it had seemed like outside. His beard and eyebrows looked bushier and the hair on his head was thick and hadn't been cut for a long time.

"The grapes of the gods," Urig said after he had taken a swaller.

"Urig hasn't got no sense," Hiwasse said. "He's read all of them books over there and it's left his head addled. Me and Urig use to bootleg together and he saved up what he made and I blowed mine, and look whur he is and whur I am."

Hiwasse was talking like Urig wasn't even there. Urig looked around the room with a kind of squint to his eyes except when he was helping hisself to a drink of whisky.

"Of course one thing I've still got," Hiwasse went on, "is a little bit of sense. Urig ain't got none. I wouldn't start in on a bootleg deal with him now for nothin. He's awright to handle a gas pump but not to bootleg. That takes everday sense."

Tucky had put down her magazine and shut off her

radio and was giving all of her attention to Urig. She looked like she didn't know what to think of him and I knowed she might be setting in my lap any minute.

"We had some good times together though, didn't we, Urig?"

Urig brought his hands together in his lap and crossed his legs. "Time," he said, "is the element we live by. I was born in time and will die in time. So will you. Time and chance happens to all of us. Out out candle."

"See what I mean?" Hiwasse said. "He knows everthing we're sayin. Don't nothin not go in his head. It's what comes out of his mouth. Hell, if he hadn't of started to read them books me and him could be livin off of the fat of the land."

I hated to ask about Urig with him setting there but it seemed to be all right so I said, "What kinds of books does he read?"

"Hell, I don't know. Ones like them over there," Hiwasse said, pointing to the bookshelf.

I went over to the shelf and looked and some of the titles was these: *Shakespeare, Thesaurus, Five in a Bed, Mythology, The Bible, Strange Sex Habits, Familiar Quotations, O. Henry, Information Please Almanac, Principles of Economics, Gang-Bang in Harlem, Twilight Girls, The Dictionary,* and so forth. They was a lots more.

"Does he talk funny to the folks he waits on," I said, "that buys gas and sech?"

"Sometimes he talks awright. Say somethin that ain't out of them books, Urig."

Urig turned his head like it was run by machine and looked at Hiwasse.

194

"I took in fourteen dollars in the last hour," he said. "Some of it in gas and some in oil."

Then Urig went back to squinting.

"See what I mean?" Hiwasse said.

"How come he's got all of that hair?" I wanted to know.

"He taken that from the Bible and figgers it gives him strenth in bed. He brags he can do more in a night than I can do in a week. Haw. Says he goes over to a certain house and can take on the whole works, includin the nigger clean-up woman. All between midnight and daylight."

Hiwasse leaned over and give him a punch on the shoulder. "Ain't that so, Urig?"

"That's so," Urig said, "and I can do better'n that. I can redo what I've done."

Hiwasse let out a holler like he was a happy Indian about to scalp somebody.

Tucky come running to me and I said, "Tucky, don't pay Hiwasse no mind."

Hiwasse said, "Nah, Tucky. That there was a laugh."

"Are we among disbelief?" Urig wanted to know.

"We're among a liar," Hiwasse said. "Here, have some more of this whisky, Urig, and pass it on to Rover."

Hiwasse commenced to tell Urig all about the adventures that me and him and Tucky had went through. He made up a few things but he stuck to the facts most of the time. When Hiwasse got to the part about the niun and the nail and me being the Lord Jesus Youngblood, Urig showed a lot of interest and stopped squinting.

"You better watch it," Urig said. "They're liable to get you, them IIIUNERS. They had a book-burning here in Manfred City about a week ago. They'll like as not get my books there on the shelf."

"They ain't studyin them books," Hiwasse told him, "when they got somebody like me that might take out after all their wives. And you talk about all that hair of yorn." Hiwasse give a big laugh.

"What I'm studyin about," I said, "is lookin fer a job. I wanta try to make somethin outa myself."

I figured whether I turned out to be Lord Jesus or Rover I was still gonna have to put food in my mouth.

"They's lots of time," Hiwasse said. "Now's when you oughta rest. Ain't that so, Urig? Have another drink."

Hiwasse had a big drink first and then another one and then handed the bottle to me.

"Hiwasse," I said, "you're shorely gonna land on yore face in a little bit."

He said, "Me? Nah." Then he commenced to rock big and rocked forward and right onto his face. I waited for him to move but he didn't."

Urig got up and leaned him against the rocker and there he set with his head hanging down.

"He can hold much of the wine of the gods," Urig said, "but not all of it." He started to play with his beard by wrapping it around his fingers, then pulling it apart in the middle and then putting it back together. I wondered to myself if it did give him all that strenth in bed, and I wondered if he was to cut it off if maybe he couldn't do nothing. It seemed bad to have to depend on your hair because they was so

many things that could happen to it. Of course something could happen to any part of you but most of
the vital parts was more protected.

"Hiwasse'll be awright," I said. "He ain't had nothin
much to eat today. Me and Tucky ain't either. Have we,
Tucky?"

All Tucky done was shaken her head. I could tell
she didn't want to say nothing much around Urig.

"What got you to readin all them books?" I asked
him.

"The Search," he said and he said it so quick it made
me think he must of give that answer before.

I thought about asking him what kind of a search it
was, for gold or silver or what, but decided not to.

He turned and looked at me straight on.

"Tell me about that nail you've got."

"Well," I said, "I got it here in my pocket. It first
belonged to the Lord Jesus Turner and was then give
to me by the Virgin Mary Turner. You can look at it
but I can't let you tech it."

I pulled it out and held it up.

"Does it make you the Lord Jesus?" he said and
sounded like he meant it. He didn't smile or nothing
when he said it.

"Hit do!" Tucky said while I was still studying what
to say.

Urig asked me, "What can you perform with it?"

"Right offhand I don't know," I told him.

"That would be correct," Urig said. "If you was
truly the Lord Jesus there wouldn't be calling for you
to perform miracles just because you wanted to."

The way Urig talked it was like they wasn't nothing

197

that got him much excited one way or another. He made you think of a machine that was talking. The only time he seemed excited was when they was talk about the IIIUN.

It didn't take long to get use to his ways, even when he come out with something peculiar like "What's in a name?" He wasn't nothing compared to the Lord Jesus Turner, or to the Virgin Mary who would shift back and forth from one entire person to another. He wasn't nothing bad like Willie Joe Crawford or the man with long hair that got killed.

Urig seemed peculiar but gentle and he was easy for me to get use to.

"How long you and Hiwasse been knowin each other?" I asked.

"Hiwasse wouldn't believe in the Lord Jesus, if it was you or anybody else. He believes in the Cherokee spirits."

Tucky come over and set down beside me on the floor.

I wondered to myself what kind of a answer that was that Urig had give me.

"Time is of the utmost," Urig said.

"Yessir," was all I could think of.

"About five years," Urig said. "We worked for a while on the other side of Manfred City. Made us some money."

He was pulling apart his beard again like it was two curtains and he was squinting.

"The Search goes from the outer to the inner. Whisky is inner. Sex is inner."

I decided from them words that I wasn't going to find out much about his and Hiwasse's dealings. I thought maybe I'd like to get to be a bootlegger myself, except that ma would drop dead. As far as being the Lord Jesus was concerned, the Lord Jesus Turner had did all right with his homebrew.

"Mr. Urig," I said, "they's somewhur in Manfred City I wanta go this evenin to see about gettin a job and other things. I wonder if it's close to here." I studied in my head for the name of the street and number that Ursula had give me. "It's 188 Malburn Street and I'm suppose to see Miss Delia."

Urig's head come around to look at me, still like it was run by machine but a whole lots faster at turning. He lost the squint and seemed like he knowed something about what I was talking about.

"Uh huh," he said. "You know that street and that number and do you know Miss Delia?"

I told him I didn't know Miss Delia at firsthand but somebody had told me to see her.

"Uh huh. Delia, Delia, who is Delia?"

I told him I didn't know except I was suppose to see her.

"It ain't far to where she lives," he told me, and now he was squinting again. "Not far when you reckon the distance to stars and eternity."

I told him I wasn't reckining on that kind of distance but was thinking about how far Bessie could take me and us not be all night at it.

"You can't ride that horse to Miss Delia's," he said. "No. You might get spotted by IIIUN. They might trace you back here. They might burn my books. No, you can't ride that horse."

"Is it too fer to walk?" I asked him.

"You still might get spotted by the ɪɪᴜɴ. I'll take you myself in my pickup truck. I'll steal you away in the dead of night."

I told him I didn't think it would be all of that dangerous.

"This is the way I plan it," he started out. "I'll put you in the back of my pickup, throw a piece of tarpaulin over you, like you was a sack of chicken feed, and then I'll drive normal, about fifteen to twenty miles an hour, first going down Partee Street, then cutting across left. That's the best way." He waited a minute. "In times like these, percaution is a must. Even the trees have ears."

I wasn't worried about the trees and I wasn't worried about anything else half as much as it sounded like Urig was. The only thing, he didn't seem to be as worried as he let on.

"When you reckin we can get started?" I asked him.

"Be in no haste," he said and had him some whisky.

I said to Tucky, "Now you stay here with Hiwasse while I'm gone and take care of him and that radio. Won't be nothin to hurt you. Hiwasse'd probly wake up if you throwed some water on him. Anyhow this here door is marked PRIVATE, so you'll be all right. Won't she, Mr. Urig?"

"The nigger child will be in the hands of God," he answered.

"The colored child," I said before Tucky had got a chance.

"Colored though she be."

"And listen here, Tucky," I went on, "I'll try and find you and Hiwasse somethin to eat. Awright?"

200

She nodded her head and pulled the radio up to her body.

Then I remembered Bessie and said, "I need to get some water fer my hoss."

Urig told me he didn't want me out there with Bessie where somebody might spot me and that he'd have it took care of. He ended up by saying, "A horse, a horse, my kingdom for a horse."

I said, "You shore can't beat a hoss, not by no piece of machinery."

Urig give me his plans which was these:

He'd drive his pickup to the back of the station where they was a door that I could slip out of. The tarpaulin would be ready in the back of the pickup. He'd be standing by the cab of the truck cleaning his fingernails and letting on like they wasn't nothing happening. Then I was to zip out and zip under the tarpaulin and lay there.

Before he started up he'd look around like he was looking for a airplane or something and try to spot if anybody was watching. If they wasn't anybody he'd start the pickup and go along the direction he'd already told me about.

When we got to 188 Malburn Street he'd let me know if it was safe by starting to sing "The Star-Spangled Banner." If it wasn't safe he'd sing "Yankee Doodle Dandy."

"Have you got all that clear in your head?" he asked me.

I told him I did. I couldn't see no sense in it but I thought I might as well go along with it. As roundabout as it was it seemed like the quickest way to get where I was going.

201

"When I leave this room," Urig told me, "you count to one hundred. Then you march out of this room, close the door, turn to your left, and you'll see another door. Go to that door, open it, and there'll be the pickup."

"Awright," I said.

"The gods go with you, Lord Jesus." Then he left the room.

"Tucky, I gotta start countin, so you may as well turn on yore radio."

"Hit ain't nothin gonna hurt you, is hit?" Tucky said.

"Naw," I told her. "I'm the Lord Jesus."

She turned on the radio to the news and I started to count.

When I got to a hundred I done just like Urig said, and sure enough there he was cleaning his fingernails by the cab of the truck. We started up a few minutes after I'd got under the tarpaulin. It was so hot under there I thought I might smother to death and not never see Manfred City.

We drove along as slow as Urig said we would. After while I commenced to hear all kinds of noises of automobiles, horns and brakes being put on and other rackets. I decided I was gonna take a look to see what Manfred City was all about, and I done it.

It was a sight I couldn't believe, what with all of the automobiles and stores and especially all of the lights that was so many different colors, pink and blue and red and yellow and so forth. It come up to looking as purty as any sunset I'd ever saw at Clearpoint. In fact it looked more like the pictures you'd see on a calendar.

I was looking out from the edge of the tarpaulin, laying on my belly and in no kind of comfort, but that

202

didn't matter to me none. Ever kind of odd feeling was going through my body at seeing and hearing the likes of all that was around me.

"Rover," I said to myself out loud, "look what all they is you got to learn about. Ain't it a sight? Now who would swap all of this here fer bein the Lord Jesus Youngblood? You'd have to go around blessin things and actin sanctimonious and tellin people they was right and wrong and settin all kinds of examples. If you're the Lord Jesus, it ain't worth it."

What with that, I reached down in my pocket and taken the nail and dropped it out the back end of the pickup. And there went the end of Lord Jesus Youngblood.

I thought to myself, What if that nail causes somebody to have a puncture?

I could see the pore unexpecting man pulling it out of a tire and having to be the next Lord Jesus Whoever.

Chapter 15

JUST A FEW MINUTES after the pickup stopped I heard Urig commence to sing, "Oh, say can you see," and he was singing it loud enough to get the attention of the IIIUN or anybody else that might be in that part of Manfred City. Urig didn't have a good singing voice besides the fact that he wasn't putting no tune to the words.

When I got off of the truck he told me, "That's it," and pointed to a great big two-story house that didn't seem to have no lights on anywhere except for a little one about as big as your thumb at the front door.

"Don't look like nobody's at home," I said.

"Yeah, somebody's home all right. You hurry up. I'll wait here in the truck. Watch out you don't get spotted."

I went across the yard that didn't look like it had any grass on it but I seen some big bushes up against the house.

On the door they was a glass piece about head-high and when I knocked somebody pulled back a curtain and looked at me. I couldn't see nothing but eyes.

Then the door opened and there stood Ursula.

"Howdy, Ursula," I said.

It taken her a minute and then she said, *"Rov*er! *Fab*ulous! Come on in here."

I did, just inside a hallway where they was hats and coats and so forth.

Ursula had on some kind of a long dress that you could see through. She throwed her arms around me and we kissed.

When we was through I said, "I just got here a little bit ago to Manfred City."

Ursula said, "Fabulous. I couldn't take Tullis no longer. I couldn't take him one minute or one second longer. And whur was I gettin out yonder in the sticks. I could of dried up and blowed away. And so here I am whur I use to be, and it's like comin back from the dead."

"Well, I'm shore glad to see you," I said. "I come here to talk to Miss Delia that you was tellin me about, to see if she knowed whur I could get a job."

"She's off in the back of the house workin at her books. You can talk to me now. I want us to talk fer a long time."

I told her they was somebody waiting for me outside and that I had to get back to Tucky and Hiwasse.

205

"Send him on," Ursula said. "I'll see you're took whurever you wanta go. I can get the chief of police to take you if you want me to."

I went back to the pickup and said to Urig, "I'm gonna stay a little while."

"Uh huh," he said. "I figgered you would. I am not without wisdom, no matter the frame of my body."

I handed him some money and told him, "Buy somethin to eat fer Tucky and Hiwasse. Say I'll be back a little later on. And don't fergit to water Bessie."

"Be watchful of the holiness of the body," he said and took off.

At the door Ursula said, "Come on in here to the settin room so's we can talk. Business ain't started up yet."

I went into this here room that had four-five big deep chairs in it and it was so dim you couldn't hardly make out the floor.

I set down in a deep chair and Ursula set on my lap.

"Well, this here's home," she said, "and it's shore fabulous to be back. I brought all my records and everthing."

I said, "You got a awful big house. Is Miss Delia yore mother?"

"*Course* not. She's who I work fer." Ursula patted at my hair. "Miss Delia's a doll, and was she glad to see me back. She said all the men had been wantin to know whur I was at."

Then it finally come to my head what kind of a place I was in and what Ursula was doing there.

"Let's go on back to my room," Ursula said, "so's won't nobody bother us and we can relax." She stood up and smoothed down her dress. "I got three new records! One is Elvis! And Miss Delia's gonna buy me five LPs because I come back. She's fabulous."

We went to this room that I couldn't tell much about at first because it was dark too. I could see a record machine setting on a table.

"You lay down on the bed and rest," Ursula said, "and I'll go tell Miss Delia I want the night off so's I can be with my boy friend. I'll put on one of the new records fer you. And I'll get us a bottle of nippy-nip."

Ursula was whirling around and looked like she was sure enough happy to see me.

After she'd went out I laid down on the bed and started thinking about how good it was to be laying there and not hiding out from nobody. Then somebody come to the door and said, "Ursula?" I could make out in the dark that it was a tall woman without no clothes on.

"She ain't here," I said.

The woman come on up to the bed to where I could make her out and it was the Virgin Mary or Ava Maureen. Her face hadn't improved none.

When she'd made me out she said, "I don't want none of you! My name is Ava Maureen and I don't want none of you!"

I tried to tell her I'd throwed away the nail but she run out of the room before I got a chance to. Then I decided that maybe I'd better not let on about throwing away the nail. It might get back to Lord Jesus Turner and the ɪɪᴜɴers.

I got up and changed the record. This one was sung by what sounded like a quartet and was all about them wanting to hold this here gal's hand. That's all they was to it.

When I'd laid down again I thought to myself, Rover, tomorrow you can hit yore stride in Manfred City. They's a lots you've got to look forward to.

I decided I'd send some picture postcards back to Clearpoint and one to Miss Mary Dove.

The record commenced to go ba-zzz ba-zzz ba-zzz and then Ursula come in and said, *"Fab*ulous!"

THOMAS McAFEE, who grew up in Haleyville, Alabama, is an associate professor of English at the University of Missouri. His writing has appeared in many literary quarterlies, anthologies, and magazines, including *Esquire, Prairie Schooner, Transatlantic Review, Compass Review,* and *The Beloit Poetry Journal.*
ROVER YOUNGBLOOD, his first novel, is his third published book. It was preceded by *Poems & Stories* (1960) and *I'll Be Home Late Tonight* (1967), a collection of poetry.

DATE DUE

NOV 26 84			
DEC 29 84			
AUG 10 85			
DEC 12 1986			
JAN 19 '87			
OCT 17 '87			
AUG 20 1999			
GAYLORD			PRINTED IN U.S.A.